The Sabotaged GIRL

A Fictional Story based on Real Life

By Dionne Simpson

The Sabotaged Girl

Authored by Dionne Simpson

www.marciampublishinghouse.com

TABLE OF CONTENTS

CHAPTER 1
Life with a limp

A buse is a difficult topic for anyone to process, whether a victim, witness, or supporting someone who has experienced abuse.

We read stories in the news, hear anecdotal evidence from family, friends or colleagues but it only goes a little way to understanding the experience of the abused.

Something often expressed is, "but how could this happen?" A good question, without a simple answer but something I will attempt to shed some light on for you.

You see, some girls and women are born into circumstances which, through no fault of their own, leave them vulnerable to abuse. No, I am not blaming victims for their own abuse. What I am stating is that childhood shapes our perspective of love and relationships.

Family relationships and those early interpersonal dynamics leave an indelible mark on the soul, imprinting us with hidden messages about our worth, value and abilities, even before we have time to develop a sense of 'self' or 'I'.

We are raised to believe it is our duty to serve others through motherhood and homemaking. Provide emotional stability for men and children, and meet the unrealistic sexual fantasies created by boys and men, all the while appearing virginal, subservient, and aesthetically pleasing to others.

We carry this burden from a young age, with gender bias imprinted on the colour of our clothes, the bows, curls, and shiny shoes intended to increase our "desirability" and restrict our behaviours to separate us from our male counterparts by the time we are toddlers.

All girls and women have experience of gender bias to varying degrees with disparities caused by the intersectionality of race, religion, geography, culture, and disability to name a few. However, for abused girls and women, there can be other factors that contribute to their vulnerability.

Here are the things which contributed to my own personal vulnerabilities. Have you ever had a stone in your shoe that wasn't painful enough for you to remove your shoe because you were in a hurry? This is a bit like that. We are all journeying through life, towards our personal destinations, but some of us are going to experience handicaps along the way, making the experience a little more uncomfortable, and for some, outright painful. In fact, by the time you arrive, you will probably have a limp, and the world will tell you how the pain is normal and you shouldn't complain. Minimising your experience before you have had time to process the pain yourself.

Pebble Number One

For a fully interactive experience, find a small pebble and put it in your shoe. Go on! I want you to experience in a small way how a person can become vulnerable to abuse, even before their life has really started. Now stand up, and just stay there, while you read all about stone number one.

I now have the benefit of hindsight, age and wisdom which has allowed me to share a perspective that I did not have when I was experiencing abuse.

I grew up assuming I had an idyllic childhood because I didn't know any different (not an uncommon experience). We lived in the countryside, and I loved school. I was inseparable from my best friend who was also my sister. We had long summers, family days out, and spent regular time with our extended families, building forever friendships with cousins and aunties.

I can't say that we did all the normal stuff other kids did, but at the time it didn't seem strange. I was told we had a good life, and that we were lucky. For many years, I just assumed that was the truth.

My earliest memories are mixed at best. I can see my dad shouting at my baby sister for not eating pizza. She wasn't even a year old yet. I was two years older than her, and already starting to notice uncomfortable issues in life.

I remember my sister crying because our dad had been away for a few days and brought me a gift back from his travels. He didn't get my sister anything, which devastated her. This was something he did often. Favouring me while treating her like she didn't exist.

Our home was always filled with music and singing with old-time church songs, soul and Motown being our mum's favourites. We would all dance around our tiny dining room as if the rest of the world didn't exist, blotting out the realities of life for a few stolen moments.

Then it all changed.

Our dad was gone, without any proper goodbye or explanation. In fact, by the time we realised his absence, he had apparently been gone for a few weeks. Our mum cried a lot. In fact, that's what I remember the most. Waking up early in the morning to find her on the floor by the fire, sobbing her heart out. As a child you don't imagine that parents cry. You think they are indestructible superheroes, who know everything and can save you from everything. For me, that myth was shattered by the age of five.

It got even harder after that. My mum and sister both hated my dad. The mention of his name would make the air get cold. I tried to get comfort when I missed him, but all I got were nasty comments about how he left me and didn't want me. That didn't matter to me. I just missed my dad, as many children in similar positions do.

We wrote letters that were never replied to, and for a few years, we were all a little broken. A little sore. A little less.

We did see lots of family though. Church was the one staple in our lives, and although we didn't get it, we loved it! We got to see our cousins, aunts, and grandparents, and at the end of church, we got to have one of the stale biscuits our gran always kept in her handbag.

Church back then was a thing to behold. We went to a Pentecostal Church of God. Black people church!

I don't recall ever having seen a white person there, but at my young age it wasn't something I really thought about (unless others brought it up). Looking back now, it was as stereotypical as you could get.

Hats for women were a must and as a young girl, I couldn't wait to be old enough to wear my first hat. It was like the black church equivalent of a Bar Mitzvah, but without the ceremony. It was also an unconscious way to control the female gender using culture and religion to mask the blatant gender inequality that was considered normal at the time.

Home was just an extension of church, with family prayer meetings, children's bible study, and always an air of watching and waiting for God to do something amazing.

Life was full of little miracles. Debts being cleared, transport or money being provided, and our needs being met. As a young child, it never occurred to me that God may not exist, that miracles sometimes didn't happen and that not everyone lived their lives in the midst of the supernatural.

Although we never talked about it much, our dad leaving, left a mark on us all. My sister became a social introvert, only speaking when spoken to and, even then, not always. She was different with me and the hurt caused by our dad's departure seemed to bring us closer together. With me she was open, talkative, and loved to tell stories. It didn't matter if I wasn't interested or not listening; she carried on regardless. I think it was her way of escaping the pain that life brought us at such an early age.

For me it was different. I seemed outwardly to cope and adjust to our new life circumstances, but my psyche gave me away. I wet the bed until the age of nine, which certainly told a different story than the one I told others and myself.

For a girl, your father is your first experience of being loved by someone outside of yourself. Your first experience of someone choosing to love you and the blueprint for your lovers of the future. My first love abandoned me, neglected my sister, and broke my mother's heart.

Pebble Number Two

How do you feel so far? I bet it's getting a bit uncomfortable standing on that little stone! We are not done yet. Go ahead and add another pebble in your shoe. Shift it around if you like, to try to find that sweet spot where it won't bother you too much. I already know that in the end, it won't matter, but I'll let you try.

Are you standing uncomfortably? Then we'll begin!

Pebble number two came wrapped in a miracle. You know the kind where you believe that something this amazing had to be magic. Or in our case, Almighty God had answered our prayers.

My sister and I had been taught to pray. It's one of the things that kept us together, kept us sane and helped us cope. We had knelt on the floor next to our handmade bunk beds and asked God for a new dad. He could do that, right? If he could part the Red Sea, bring Jesus back to life, and send rain to flood the earth, this would be easy. Well, he did it or, at least, that's what we thought.

Our mum brought him home one day for us to meet. A skinny, long-haired biker, with spray-on jeans and cowboy boots. His eyes were covered by thick, dark-lensed glasses and he hada cowboy shirt with long tassels.. I can't recall how I felt about him at the time, but I do know that we found it amusing to have this strange man in our home.

It was like my mum had brought an alien into our house. We had only ever been around a few white men in our short lives, and most of those were teachers at school. However, this was entirely different.

It didn't take long for us to realise that he was not used to being around children. He seemed to think that shouting was the only communication we understood, but it was always about random things like, "Get ready for bed!" but bellowed at us using his scariest man voice. We frequently had to hide our fits of laughter at his faltering attempts to parent us.

Mum was happy though. She met him at a local barn dance (no, I was not born in the 1800s) and like I said, we were country folk, and that's what passed as entertainment back then.

It all happened very quickly, within a year they were married and we had a new dad. My sister and I were ecstatic that God had answered us, and our family entered its honeymoon phase.

During this honeymoon phase, many changes occurred. This is not uncommon with newly blended families. Everyone had to find their new position, and sodid we.

However, this process brought new rules, restrictions and expectations which, looking back, were disproportionately detrimental to the women in my family. Church, home and school became the only places we were permitted to go. At the time, this did not seem odd, after all, we were used to that. But what made it oppressive was the exclusion of all other things that madeup a normal social life.

The TV was the first to go. The revival of God in our house meant that TV was the window to the world, a distraction from God and implanted the seeds of sin in the soul. This also went for all books, magazines and any written media. Nothing was allowed in the house that hadn't been pre-approved by our parents or our church.

At one point, even Christmas and Christmas trees were banned from our home because they were a pagan tradition. We were told that demons lived in the trees, once worshipped by our archenemy. Non-believers!

We lived in fear of demonic influence, that would obviously penetrate our holy home (through the Christmas tree) and lead us into sin or demon possession of some sort. Living with adults who not only believed this, but indoctrinated us with the same beliefs, made for a scary upbringing, dominated by fear. We did not need scary stories at Halloween. We lived in fear every day.

I know on paper it doesn't seem like an entirely harmful thing but let me explain the impact. We were starved of basic knowledge and knew nothing of current affairs, politics, wars, pop music, soap operas, children's TV programmes, fashion, or public opinion.

This kept us excluded from engaging with kids our own age at school. Other kids were singing the latest pop songs, chatting about popular kids TV and sharing elements of popular culture that we had never even heard of. Non-uniform day was a nightmare and another example of how gender inequality was part of our everyday life. Our religious family zealously followed strict rules about what girls and women could wear. Dressing modestly was taken to the extreme.

We grew up in the 1980's and the fashion was distinct. While most girls turned up in leg warmers, layered skirts, neon socks, and crimped hair, my sister and I rocked the latest Amish-wear. We never wore trousers, as these were considered 'men's' clothing and a sin according to our church.

Instead, we were provided with a velvet pinafore dress made with a heavy velvet, calf-length skirt with a stitched-on blouse, complete with frills on the cuffs, collar, and covering the buttons down the front. It was almost unbearable and made us the laughing stock of the whole school. Add that to the fact we were two of only four black children attending an all-white school, which made us an even bigger target for abuse and bullying.

During conversations about the latest drama on a TV soap, we were nonplussed. School reports about the Gulf War and politics were not completed as we couldn't watch the news, read newspapers, or have any way of finding out what was happening in the world. But what we did have was a proud knowledge of the Holy Bible, access to regular preaching of sermons, a wild distrust of 'The World' and a healthy fear of sinning and going to hell.

Hell was another prominent feature growing up and was used to instil a healthy dose of fear and obedience during our childhood. Any deviation from authoritarian demands was met with hellfire. Punishment and repentance for perceived or actual wrongs was dealt out swiftly and often with corporal punishment. We were repeatedly told that if we went to sleep without being forgiven for our sins, we might miss the rapture as Jesus was sure to come back when we were asleep or in the bath, or some other time when we were not ready.

This ever-looming high-level threat and fear, was something we lived with daily. Fear was our friend; it kept us safe, protected us from sin and helped us walk the narrow path of the Lord. Or at least, that's what we were told.

To say we were the weird and lonely kids at school would have been an astute assessment, yet it didn't end there.

Home became a place of crazy demands, expectations and rules. We didn't know why and were not allowed to ask. Questions were like forbidden fruit and if you dared to eat it, it resulted in sin and further corporal punishment. Punishment was like food in our house. It was considered a form of nourishment, because God only punishes those he loves. If that's true we were loved a lot in our house.

For us, it quietly bred fear, compliance, silence and a deep desire not to die in the fires of hell.

As if that wasn't bad enough, we were taught to be grateful. After all, there were people far worse off than us, and our righteous duty was to serve, love, and care for the people around us. Another gender-based responsibility thrust upon us as young girls, which alongside our restricted lifestyle, created an unconscious noose of servitude, that kept us trapped in a cycle of subservience, pleasing others and neglecting ourselves. A perfect breeding ground for abuse.

My sister and I grew up with no sense of self, were stripped of personal desires, and ignorant of the world we were supposed to live in. We knew nothing about regular relationships, lacked any common knowledge, and regularly lived at bomb-threat levels of unhealthy fear that kept us silent.

This, coupled with our parents' insatiable need to move house, towns, and cities, more times that we can remember, left us isolated and vulnerable. The worst thing was, we didn't even know it. We grew up believing we were privileged, blessed and with a holy mission to save the world.

The reality is that we were brainwashed into believing we had no choices, that bad things would happen if we didn't comply and even love from our parents was conditional.

Pebble Number Three

Friendship is a funny thing. We all seem to think that we know what a friend is, yet when you ask, most people will have completely different answers. Before I tell you what I think a real friend is, I want to share my lifetime experiences of friendship.

As a child, friendship is a simple thing. There are few expectations. You spend time together, play, laugh, and care. There may be just the two of you or more. During my childhood I had very few friends but seemed to know everybody. I was never shy and always upfront and outspoken. My confidence allowed me to spend time with almost anyone, without ever getting close enough that any real commitment was made.

Being a black child in a white neighbourhood was challenging enough. Racial taunting was usual, but most kids got bored when they realised, I was a fighter. This helped my 'street cred' no end. I only had one real friend at school. I thought she was beautiful and intelligent, but her friends always made me feel that I was unwanted. I was invited by my friend to hang out (on the rare occasions my parents would allow it), but her friends would deliberately go to places they knew I was not allowed, or would change their plans and not tell me, just to ditch me. Typical mean girls, but that is how children are sometimes.

My life was a steady constant of church and school, with not much else in between. This meant my main friendships were born from those environments. I had two best friends at church: Dale and Martin. They were cousins and about five years my senior. They were great fun. My black skin never bothered them, they kept our dates and were always pleased to see me. They attended our church, so my parents were happy to allow me some freedom if it was in their company. Being devoid of any other friendships in my life, I clung to these particularly hard. I honestly thought they would be my friends forever. Sadly, life has a way of shattering childlike dreams.

At the age of 15, an incident in our church pushed Martin to the point of deciding to turn away from church and God. I was heartbroken. The funny thing is it was completely selfish. I wasn't sad that he lost his faith. I was devastated that my only friend in the world would no longer be in my life. I had lost someone precious to me, and in my mind, he could never be replaced. Soon after that, Dale stopped calling and my short-lived forever-friendship died in front of my eyes.

My parents moved yet again, and we were in a new town, in a new house, in new schools and everything changed. Back to being lonely, friendless and having to start all over again on this treadmill of attempted social life.

It was many, many years before I once again found true friendship.

The family move became a trigger. I was already hurt and grieving my loss and blamed my parents for destroying the only truly happy thing I had that was mine. Add to that feeling being betrayed by our church family, who had succeeded in destroying the hearts and minds of its congregation. Teenage rage and despondency had well and truly set in.

At the tender age of 15 years old, I ran away from home knowing that what they claimed to be love was nothing but a lie. I felt unsafe, unloved, and disillusioned by the only people that I knew. I decided that anything had to be better than this and by leaving, for the first time, made a decision for myself.

As liberating as this sounds, it was a short step out of the fire and into the frying pan. I quickly met a man much older than myself, who preyed on my vulnerabilities and exploited my limited knowledge of people, relationships, and the world.

These pebbles are the foundation stones of my life but also a reflection of the experiences many girls and women go through. How do you feel? Are the stones like knives in your soles yet? Can you run, walk, or hop at your leisure? What are your pain levels like? Do you have a high tolerance or are you at breaking point?

This is how I started life. Limping from the pebbles inherited by my upbringing. I was operating from a deficit but never understood why. I was totally blind to the impact of these events on the rest of my life. These pebbles became the perfect breeding ground for what came next.

I hope that this simple analogy goes some way to highlighting some of the vulnerabilities that we can acquire in childhood. It can make us easy prey for those who choose to abuse, bully, and subjugate in relationships.

It can take many years to decode childhood vulnerabilities and for some of us, this is a lifelong pursuit. What I hope you take away is that we all have them to a greater or lesser degree. And that vulnerable girls and women are at greater risk of falling prey to predatory behaviours because of gender inequalities, social and cultural expectations and poor expressions of love from an early age.

The Sabotaged Girl is a fictional story based on the real events of women and girls just like me.

CHAPTER 2
You see me

Donna had spent more than a decade losing at life, finally ending up at Victory House rehab centre. She had to face the uncertainty of leaving with the end of her programme looming.

Her new challenge was to attempt to create something that did not resemble the trauma and bad decisions of her early life, which was never going to be easy.

During her time at the rehab, Donna was constantly challenged about things she did not even realise were problems. They highlighted her ignorance about herself, but in a gentle and caring way. They were the only people she had opened up to in many years, building trust she had not experienced in a long time.

Even though she was only there for a short time, they became a monumental part of her growth and influenced her in ways she could never have predicted. The teaching and support she received formed a new foundation for her life and enabled her to grow and develop as she journeyed through life.

Donna was so proud to celebrate the commitment and hard work of the staff at Victory House ladies' rehab. Her faith in God grew, hearing stories of the many transformed and renewed lives who had passed through over the years, including hers. Donna quietly prayed that their ministry would continue to love, support and develop hurting women for many years to come.

It had been many eventful years since Donna had left Victory House, and she felt a need to reconnect, so she started to write a diary to help her reflect on her journey. Her first entry was a letter to her old counsellor, Alicia.

Hi Alicia,

Aside from wanting to touch base with you, I really wanted an opportunity to share some things I have been exploring. As you know, I struggled to clearly recollect or acknowledge many things which happened before arriving at Victory House.

You clearly identified some traumas and pains that I simply wasn't ready to address while I was with you. I look back on our time together wishing that I had more time to spend in your counsel and listen to your guidance and wisdom once more.

God has been faithful and seen me through some very hard times, as I am sure he has with you too. He has helped me to uncover some tragedies of the past, some long-forgotten traumas and helped me to reflect, forgive, and make peace with the injustices and poor decisions thrust upon me.

I always thought I went to Victory House to get clean from drugs, but now I know, it was so much more than that. God finally had me in a place where he could begin to uncover the real me.

You saw me, long before I could see myself. You never rushed to expose my hidden parts, but gently coached me to dig deeper into God. This gradually opened my eyes, which had been darkened by life.

You were patient, kind and challenging without ever being harsh. These are the things I have carried with me, that I continue to develop and have allowed me to safely venture into my past, safe in the knowledge that God is there to heal and not to harm.

For this, I am eternally grateful, and you will forever have a special place in my heart. I thank God for allowing you, to invest in me.

Keep helping women to be overcomers.

In kindness

Donna

CHAPTER 3
R-E-S-P-E-C-T

Respect is something that I never learned about as a child. I knew I had to respect others but that was mostly a tool for control.

All I knew was forced compliance gained by dominance and abuse. I never knew I needed to respect myself and it caused me to make some of the worst decisions of my life.

Self-respect is subtle and less talked about when the topic of 'respect' arises. My experiences have taught me that our level of self-respect influences our decisions. We can be uplifted and encouraged by God's truth about us or be tricked by lies and manipulation which keep us downtrodden or trapped. The enemy wants to destroy our self-respect and uses other people to do his dirty work.

The truth is that we are precious, loved children of God. Each of us is uniquely created by his hand in his image and loved unconditionally. This is where our true self-respect should lie. Not in the actions of our daily lives, but in believing what God thinks of us.

Over the many years that I lived without a relationship with God, I had many experiences that shattered my self-respect. I know the rehab councillors already knew this from first-hand experience. They had seen many girls and women like me, devastated by our emotional wounds, leaving us to be swallowed up by false beliefs, forced upon us by those wanting to control us.

I can't believe I was so deceived (it's almost embarrassing). Not because of my poor self-worth, but because I completely refused to acknowledge the true impact of my traumas. It's like positive post-traumatic stress disorder. Instead of having flashbacks of terrible ordeals, I had painted over them completely with false memories, minimised the impact and forced myself into a fake happiness, which permeated every part of my mind.

I started out as a young woman, raised in a loving Christian home, and taught all the principles of living a Christian life. At the age of 15, after a culmination of family strife, church fractures and lost hope, I decided God was not the way. I quickly met a man much older than myself (by 13 years), who showed me a world I had never seen before.

He was fun, exciting, fearless, and nothing like I had ever encountered. My fundamentalist Christian parents had kept me and my siblings so restricted over the years, I literally didn't know what people outside our home did. It was like being released from bondage after a lifetime of shackles, and I wasted no time in exploring and sampling everything I could, over those fun and chaotic years.

Grant was already in a relationship with two other women when we met. He didn't have an ounce of shame (something my home was always filled with) and his approach to life was refreshing and amazing to a newly released teen, who was seeing alternative lifestyles for the first time.

Any woman with an ounce of self-respect would have demanded monogamy. But my already low self-worth deceived me into accepting the situation. I believed that what others wanted was always a priority, and that my needs and wants were not important.

We had been taught so much about sacrifice, picking up our cross and accepting suffering as a gift, that it seemed completely natural to apply these pseudo-Christian beliefs to my new life. It's obvious looking back, that I was not valued or respected. Unfortunately, I had nothing but twisted religious principles instilled in me and I had nothing else to compare it to. Accepting this lack of respect, laid a foundation which twisted my thinking for many years to come.

I moved in with Grant to a shared house with lots of people, parties, and drugs. I had never heard of drugs, so when offered various substances I had no reason to say no. That is how I ended up taking heroin from the age of 15.

To me, Grant was everything I ever wanted. He gave me the freedom that was prohibited at home, access to 'the world' which I had never seen before and the promise of genuine friendship, which was true for the longest time. We had a gang of friends who were young, fun, unattached and a little bit wild. I absolutely loved this new world he introduced me to, and the new experiences that came with it.

It would be years before I discovered that I had been taking heroin from such a tender age. Everyone called it 'brown' and

I genuinely had no idea what it was, that drugs were bad or that they were addictive. I was naive to the point of ignorance and Grant's age made me feel safe; like another untrustworthy father figure that I longed for. So I trusted him and never gave it a second thought. It would eventually become the downfall of our entire friend group.

Looking back, I don't know how I managed to stay in employment, finish my college education, and maintain a home. All the while high on one thing or another. I guess I had the benefit of youth on my side. I also think my ignorance played an important role in protecting me from some of the behaviours that accompany regular drug use. I still had no idea about addiction, so never really associated any physical or psychological symptoms with my drug use. Had I known this, I think my demise would have come far sooner than it did.

I was totally in love with Grant and planned to get married, have kids and do the whole family thing. Had I understood then, what I do now, I would have run a million miles away, and never looked back.

Instead, my young mind and innocent heart believed that a man who was old enough to be my parent, who had groomed me as a teenager with drugs, sex, and introduced me into a life of crime, was the best the world had to offer me. I actually believed that I was lucky.

I still remember being asked to delete phone numbers of drug dealers and users I hung out with, when I arrived at rehab. Even knowing that there was not a single genuine friend among them, I had grown so accustomed to their presence in my life, it still felt like a loss. I remember trying to memorise phone numbers so that I could reconnect when I got out of Victory House.

Thankfully, staff at the rehab have worked with people like me and knew the score. After a while, I forgot the numbers, forgot the people, and I was able to focus on my relationship with God. If you hadn't already figured it out, Victory House was run by Christians, supporting broken people like me and helping us find a path to healing.

Have you ever met a person you immediately bonded with? It could be a chance meeting at work or in the street, and you feel there is something between you that can't be explained or described, but you know this person is meant to be your friend. I have had that several times, and it brings joy and tears to recall the few people in my life that I have ever had that connection with.

You spend hours on the phone talking about everything and nothing. Spend all your free time together and you think you are dreaming that you have finally found a person who understands you. They get you. It is an awesome feeling.

I have learned that these relationships are sometimes not meant to last. It breaks my heart to think of the people that I have lost touch with because our jobs have changed or one of us moved away. Maybe something happened to keep us apart: a disagreement, a partner, or a decision that caused one of us pain.

For me the loss feels like losing someone in death and it never gets easier. You have a void that cannot be filled. What do you do when you have done everything in your power to keep a special friendship alive, but it has died or been brought to an end regardless? This is something I still battle with, and Grant, among others, became the temporary stop-gap of my desire for intimacy.

My journey with God over the years has taught me some important lessons. A scripture that comes to mind is Ecclesiastes chapter 3. It talks about there being a time for everything. It helped me to understand that situations can bring both joy and pain. God is the author of our lives and I believe he both gives and takes friends from our lives for his own purpose. Sometimes he may reveal the reason and other times he may not. Sometimes the answer is obvious, but we refuse to acknowledge it because we are happy living a lie.

Thank God that I found my true friend, Jesus. Yes, he is the answer, and that is something I finally began to understand.

As part of my rehabilitation, I was asked to write down the characteristics of my ideal friend. I thought they were being sarcastic at the time, but my compliant nature didn't permit me to express this openly.

I was shocked to realise that Jesus matched every single characteristic I had put on my list. It took me ages to grasp this, but since doing it, my earthly friendships became much easier to deal with.

I no longer had that needy pressure to rest all my emotional hopes and dreams upon another person. I could actually rely on God to be my friend, with no fear that one day he may not be here or betray me in some way. He said he will never leave or forsake us. And I was finally at a place where I could believe it!

It's crazy looking back and realising that my lack of positive self-esteem left me vulnerable to being preyed upon. In today's terms, I would be classed as a victim of Child Sexual Exploitation (CSE). The diminishing of my boundaries left nothing to protect what little of my self-respect remained.

Once Grant and I broke up, I developed a twisted sense of freedom and began to indulge more heavily in drugs and began to mix with addicts, criminals and street workers. They had few boundaries and it seemed exciting. Dishonesty, greed, selfishness, hedonism, and dominance were commonplace among the people I spent time with.

In a strange way, I felt that being with people who were so obviously bad, gave me a false sense of being better than them, temporarily giving my self-esteem a much-needed boost. For a while I felt good about myself but unfortunately, this did not last.

It's taken me a long time, but I have finally started to 'un-romanticise' my relationship with Grant. It was hard. Grant brought me so many things I had never had before. Choices, friends, fun, a carefree life, and adventures in a world that I previously didn't know existed.

Don't get me wrong, I didn't decide to hate or blame Grant for how things turned out. That simply could not be predicted. But I was able to take the time to truly reflect upon what the relationship meant, how it influenced my future and how the enemy slips in unnoticed, to begin his reign of terror.

What I didn't know then, was that true terror was just around the corner.

CHAPTER 4
Trick of the light

After Grant, I quickly met and eventually got married to a man I thought had everything. Daemon seemed to have it all. Money, power, position, confidence, and self-worth. All the things I found attractive in a man and currently lacked in my own life. It is exactly these qualities that were later used to manipulate and control me, decimating my self-worth at the hands of this obsessive, cruel and twisted man.

At the time, as far as I could tell, Daemon was dynamite! Fast paced, charming, cash-rich, a business owner, and a slick operator who fawned over me at our first meeting. Unusually, we met at a job interview. He was interviewing me for a sales position at his company.

It was clear from that first meeting that we had chemistry, and I did my best to let him know that I wanted a job. What I later found out was that Daemon never took no for an answer. His tongue did a merry jig as he pandered, flirted and sweet-talked me back to his apartment that night. You would not have approved!

In all the bluster of activity, date nights, bars, clubs, drugs and drink, I never noticed the subtle changes taking place around me.

I wisely decided not to work for Daemon, and continued at my old sales job, but moved in with him, two weeks after we met. My slum-esque bedsit versus his city centre man-pad was a no brainer. So I willingly ended my tenancy and moved in to start my new life with him.

It started slowly at first. Things like he preferred this dress over that one. He preferred it if I would do this instead of that. It was so subtle that even an expert would have found it difficult to spot in the early days.

As a bit of a free spirit, I would still find time to go to meet with my old friends for a bit of a blowout (usually crack). This is what led to our earliest fall outs.

There were accusations and overbearing requests wanting to know who I was with, where I had been, why it had taken me so long to get back, etc. At first, I just thought it was a bit of jealousy, no harm really. I thought it was sweet and his way of showing that he really did love me.

I started to feel pressured, but I remembered the teachings of my parents who taught us to love selflessly, give excessively, and always consider others before ourselves. So that's exactly what I did. For every request or demand, no matter how unnecessary or bizarre, I committed to making sure my man was happy at all costs. After all, if I loved him, this is what I needed to do.

I wish I knew then what I know now! I never really talked about what life was like for me before rehab, and at the time,

I wasn't really able to see things clearly. I was still raw from the trauma, too confused to think clearly, and I was nowhere near strong enough to deal with the psychological fall-out.

These are some of the reasons why it takes so long to leave and be healed from abusive relationships. It damages your mind, your ability to think and crushes your ability to make sound decisions.

I didn't understand coercive control, gaslighting or the more subtle tactics of domestic abuse. I did not know what a healthy relationship looked like, so was unable to spot the signs.

I remember it took me a long time to admit that I was married under duress. Or a more straightforward term would be 'blackmailed.' It sounds crazy writing this on paper, as any other person would have told him to "do one", walked out and got on with their lives. But I didn't know how to do that.

My soon-to-be husband had discovered that my past wasn't exactly squeaky clean and threw all my belongings into black bin liners and sat and waited until I came home before ambushing me. He towered over me to deliver a simple ultimatum, 1) Marry him and live my life the way he wanted or, 2) Pick up the bin bag, leave immediately and never go back.

This was before The Matrix movie, or I would have known that when Morpheus offers Neo the choice between the red pill and the blue pill, to have definitely told him to shove the red pill where the sun doesn't shine. Sadly, that movie hadn't been released yet, and what followed, created cataclysmic levels of destruction.

I lost myself, my will, my desires and my freedom, and found myself alone and trapped in an abusive relationship of my own choosing. I had willingly allowed Daemon to control every aspect of my life, thinking that it would please him. His domineering personality soon had me believing that I was worth nothing without him. I was being whipped by constant verbal abuse, which soon led to eruptions of violence.

In some twisted way, my broken psyche believed it was right for him to dominate me this way. I was not allowed to go anywhere without him. He monitored all my phone calls, dressed me every morning and even put my make-up on for me. We worked and lived together, and I was not even allowed to go to the bathroom without him accompanying me. Urinating while being watched because someone refuses to trust you enough to go to the bathroom, is a whole new level of crazy I never knew existed.

He was still sleeping with his ex-wife. His twisted logic forced me to accept this as OK, because he was honest about it. Every weekend I would have to go upstairs after a night out, while he had sex with other women in our living room. He controlled all our money, and I was given an allowance and I had to account for every last penny.

I was cut off from my family and friends and was not allowed to spend any time with them, unless he was there to supervise. This was still not enough to stop him accusing me of infidelity, beating me when he drank (which was frequently), or verbally berating me with the most vile and venomous things I have ever heard come from the mouth of a human being.

For the longest time, I allowed this to continue. My husband had this policy that we lived by: honesty. This meant he could do whatever he wanted, as long as he told me about it. This was where my controlled upbringing really came into its own. Looking back, I realise that I had already had a lifetime of training to submit. My formative years were spent bowing to the choices and indoctrination of my parents and I didn't know how else to be. I knew I had to do the right thing and obey, but at the same time I felt alone, broken, abused and depressed. How did following God's rules result in me being trapped and abused?

Even though I wasn't actively following God, I still believed in Him. It was so confusing to me, that even when I did what I thought was right, it still somehow turned out wrong. I tried to escape Daemon several times but he made it impossible. He would threaten friends if they helped me, cut off my access to finances, spread malicious lies about me and even call the police on me, with spurious false allegations. I felt completely helpless, hopeless, silenced, and trapped by a façade of his making.

CHAPTER 5
The underneath

We had been married about two years and together for three. From the outside my life looked pretty good. Business was good, we had a nice home, a good lifestyle including at least four holidays abroad each year. Daemon bought me my first car, changed my wardrobe, treated me to meals out at least four times a week and didn't spare on buying me gifts.

From the outside looking in, I had a great life. What couldn't be seen was the underbelly of the beast. Firstly, Daemon was an alcoholic. It took me years to figure this one out, because I only saw him truly drunk on a handful of occasions. He was one of those high-functioning alcoholics who made it look like casual drinking.

I soon discovered flasks of whisky in his office drawers. I would watch him drink two bottles of red wine over a business lunch with colleagues, followed by half a box of wine, and most of a bottle of whisky during our evenings. That was then polished off with a late dance at our local club and washed down with tequila shots, beer and lines of cocaine.

On arrival home in the early hours, he would take two paracetamols before bed, wake in the morning with a large scotch, and the process would start all over again.

I did ask him about it on a few occasions early on in our relationship, and he scoffed at the notion of being an alcoholic. He was a firm believer that all addicts lived on the street, drank out of brown paper bags, couldn't hold down a job and would be committing crimes to feed their habit. He was right about one thing. He did not fit that description.

Daemon was intelligent. Not like regular intelligence, but borderline genius level. This was one of the things I found most attractive about him. We could talk for hours. He knew about so many things and could keep me entertained all night. He was the life and soul of the party, the generous giver, the fun intellectual, the work-hard, party-harder of the gang, and a force to be reckoned with.

His Irish roots gave him the lure of Lucifer, and I used to tease that he could sell ice to Eskimos. He was intense, driven and hyperactive to a level I had not encountered before. There seemed to be no pause button to his endless, boundless, need for interaction. I once watched him have three separate conversations at the same time. He had a phone in each hand and a staff member in the office, and I watched in awe as he effortlessly breezed between conversations, managing them each with pinpoint precision and even throwing in a few jokes. The man was unstoppable. He believed it. I believed it. Everyone believed it and it fed his enormous ego which eventually turned monstrous.

Daemon was a go-getter, a never-quitter who never lost. The very things that inspired me about him were the same tactics he would later use to crush me.

My new life with my new husband had started out so well but had slowly been replaced by a sort of solitary confinement with a strict guard. I never even saw it happening until it was too late.

Aside from the blackmail incident, our wedding was my first inkling that something was very wrong. Being from an Irish family, he had ten siblings including a twin brother. There was always some family drama which meant family members regularly fell out over some bemusing offence. Our wedding was no different and several strange incidents occurred, including public genital fondling between siblings, drunk and bleeding relatives (something about a cat in a tree) and a strange encounter with my new niece-in-law.

They were all disturbing, but it was the niece thing that really worried me. At the reception meal, this 17-year-old girl walked right up to me at the top table, bent over and whispered in my ear, "I should have been the one to get married because Daemon loves me." I nearly choked on my delicious Caribbean restaurant food. Surely, I misheard her, right? WTAF!

I quickly dismissed it and got on with enjoying my wedding, which ended with a night out in our favourite nightclub. This is when the drama started. This same niece insisted that she be allowed to go to the nightclub with us. Not an insane request but, given that this was the start of our honeymoon, traditionally, we would not have invited her along. After a drunken hissy fit, the family decided she should go, and her mum would collect her from our house later that night.

It should have been a simple hand-off at 2 a.m. but instead, we had a screaming, crying, teenager declaring her undying love for my new husband and refusing to leave our house. (This is where I want to add a row of shocked face emojis).

I tried everything to calm her down because she was inconsolable and believed that, because Daemon was now married, he couldn't love her anymore. I tried to keep a sensible head. The girl was drunk, loved her uncle, in a completely infatuated and unhealthy way, and this was just a teenage episode.

This was until she let slip that Daemon had taken her virginity and said he loved her. I felt sick and dizzy while trying to process this new information.

What on earth had I done? Who had I married? And this poor girl had been sexually abused by her uncle and believed it was love, and that they had a future together. Her mum and dad eventually had to drag her from our home, literally kicking and screaming. And I had to face the night in bed with what I suspected was a child abuser: my new husband.

Even though this sin was not my own, I still felt the shame and the pain. This isn't something I told many people. It's such a shame I wasn't ready to take advantage of the counselling I was offered when I was at rehab.

I had chosen blindness. I chose to forget and closed off my mind, and began to compartmentalise so I could get on with my life.

What kind of monster must I be to stay with a person like that? Did I make the ultimate trade-off? My integrity and morals in exchange for holidays and a nice house? Did I make a deal with the devil?

I never really looked at my marriage to Daemon through the eyes of my own sin before. It was easy to blame him for all the bad things, make him the scapegoat and relieve myself of any responsibility.

But the truth is, I accepted his sins and, in doing so, made them my own. Forgiving myself has been the hardest part of this whole process. It's taken a long time to come to terms with what I allowed, what I ignored, and what I chose to forget. My fear of loss kept me captive. That hole in my life where friendship or a significant other needed to be, was filled, and I thought that was the best I was ever going to get.

Outwardly, I had everything I wanted, but I knew it would cost me. I just had no idea at the time, how costly my decision would be.

CHAPTER 6
The Seer

Processing trauma in the middle of a busy life is not an easy task. It turned out my wounds still caused me pain. More pain than I cared to admit.

Even now, I am acutely aware I have never told anyone everything that had happened to me. And honestly, I don't know if I ever will. I used to question why God would allow me to go through such darkness, trial and trauma. I just couldn't understand what I had done to deserve it.

I now know that what I experienced was not the work of God, but the influence of evil. I know it sounds cheesy, and an easy way to write off the bad things that happen to us. It does not stop it from being true. Within a short time at Victory House, I began to have very vivid dreams, strange knowledge, and a sense that I was able to see beyond the everyday things of the world.

This was not the first time I had this experience. I just accepted that sometimes I would know what people were feeling. I knew their secret thoughts, presumably by some sort of osmosis, and my dreams revealed truths about circumstances I had no business knowing.

The first week I was there, I received what I believed was a message from God for another girl. I don't remember her name and we hadn't really spoken before. I just know that when I went to bed, God (or at least that's what I believed) told me about her insecurities and he had the solution that would make her weakness a strength.

I saw no reason not to tell her, so during that morning's breakfast, told her what I had heard.. What happened next was the strangest thing. I was told by a few of the staff that I wasn't allowed to do that and only staff were allowed to 'speak' in that way.

I was genuinely puzzled. Surely, if God wanted to tell this girl good things, she should be allowed to hear them?

It wasn't until many years later that I understood there was a hierarchy of spirituality within church structures. I also did not yet understand that my very existence would be a constant challenge to others.

Anyway, I digress. I was talking about why I had a target on my back from an ever-present enemy. The simple answer is that the enemy knew who I was, long before I had any idea.

I always had very vivid dreams, even as a young child. I had seen angels and what presented as monsters from the age of eight. Living in seclusion with my fundamentalist parents, there was no one to talk about it with. So I just assumed everyone had the same experience.

By 11 years old, I was having significant episodes of déjà vu, recounting conversations I had heard before. I knew what people were going to say before they said it, and knew random things like what someone would be wearing, because I had seen it before in a dream. These could all be written off as childhood fantasies and, for the longest time, I paid them very little attention.

What I had started to call 'glimpses' became less frequent, but I was always alerted to some issue of mine or someone I knew. This foreknowledge had, at times, enabled me to act and respond to things I would otherwise not have known.

For example, I remember having a dream about my sister Serena. She was distressed, and her house was drowning in rubbish. I was alerted by a sea of rubbish, flowing like a river out of her front door. Of itself, the dream was nothing special. But when I spoke to Serena to check she was OK, she absolutely was not. A personal issue had left her overwhelmed and on the verge of depression. She felt she couldn't share this pressure with anyone, because she felt a deep sense of duty (a pebble from our upbringing) and believed she should be able to cope with anything.

On another occasion, I remember freaking out at a friend of a friend who was visiting. I threatened to stab them if they didn't leave immediately. Everyone thought I was losing the plot. The truth was, I could see demons inside them and hear them hissing and spitting while distorting the face of the person they possessed. Freaked out does not come close to what I experienced that day. All I knew was whatever that thing was, there was no way it was staying in my house.

Despite my lack of relationship with God, the spiritual gifts he placed in me were obvious even back then. Unfortunately, at that time, I had no clue that these things I experienced were supernatural. To me, it was as normal as socks. Something I had always had, was always there and a part of me.

It wasn't until I arrived at Victory House and began to really hear and see from God clearer than ever, that God began to reveal who I was, who he was and who he made me to be.

It was at one of our daily church services where God opened scriptures in Ezekiel chapter 33 and used them to show me who I was. I was a seer. A bringer of God's message. A watcher on the wall and God had called me to be a prophet. Finally all the things I could see and hear which were beyond human capacity, began to finally make sense. I was so shocked that I was unable to move. The weight of the Holy Spirit had me panting in my seat, as I swirled from trying to believe the unbelievable.

This was the thing that the enemy knew, long before I did. I wholly believe that the enemy tried to crush and kill me at every opportunity, to prevent God from ever being able to use me, or the gifts he placed in me. God not only had a plan for me but gifted me in such a way that I have the potential to see beyond the natural world.

Now imagine how dangerous a woman of God can be, if she can see the works of the evil one and alert the saints to defend and protect God's kingdom? Just like Ezekiel, I am created to stand watch, to spot the enemy as he approaches, to sound the alarm and gather the children of God to defend God's work. All I can say is that I must be a serious threat!

I often joke with my family that Daemon was the son of the enemy. The strange thing is, I wouldn't be surprised if that were true.

A couple of years into our relationship, despite growing issues, we decided to start a family. I was super-excited and always knew I wanted to be a mum. After a few months of trying, we were pregnant, and that's where the happiness came to an abrupt halt.

For some reason I am yet to discover, my pregnancy turned Daemon into some sort of monster, seemingly overnight. As I could no longer drink and do the party thing, he began drinking ferociously and had taken to giving me beatings in the middle of the night. The next day, he would wake with no recollection of the events, leaving me in physical and emotional pain and with nowhere to lay the blame. I wasn't going to get an apology from a man with no memory of abusing me. And he made it seem childish to expect him to be sorry for something he didn't remember.

Within two months, the beatings, verbal abuse and threats were almost nightly. The final straw for me was being hauled and dragged down the hall kicking and screaming at 3 a.m. All the while begging and pleading with Daemon to stop, wake up and realise what he was doing. It was like he wasn't there, just his empty vessel possessed by a darkness I did not recognise.

I fought to get free, but it was too late. I was tumbling headfirst down a wood and cast-iron spiral staircase. I was stopped by the corner of a wall on the floor below, and I remember wailing but nothing coming out of my mouth. It was a weird silent scream.

Before I had time to catch my breath, Daemon was on me again. He grabbed my arm and started to drag me down the next flight of stairs. All I could see were my legs trailing behind me as I tried to use my free arm to get some sort of grip. There was one last tug on my arm and my whole body slipped easily down the remaining polished stairs.

I lay there, not moving, not screaming. For the first time in my life, I was scared. Really scared. I was scared that he would kill me. I was scared he would kill our unborn child. I was scared to stay, but I was also scared to leave. I had little to no contact with my family. All my money was kept by Daemon. I worked at the same office, so I would have no job if I walked out.

I had tried to leave so many times before and failed every time. He would cut my mobile phone off so I couldn't get in touch with anyone. He would call anyone I knew and threaten them if they tried to help me. He would block my bank card so I couldn't access the little money I was allowed to have.

The police were no help. Each time I called, my sweet-talking, white Irish husband would ply them full of stories about my violent behaviour, my drug habit, and how he was doing his best to deal with me. All I could do was sit and watch while he fabricated lies about his troubled black wife, which were lapped up by prejudiced police who never took the time to talk to me.

I knew I had to save the life growing inside my belly. I was only two months pregnant but had dreamed that it was a boy, and his name was Reece. I hadn't even had my first scan, but I knew it was a little boy growing in my belly. I knew he was mine and I had to do whatever it took to keep him safe from this nightmare.

I packed a bag with some essentials, grabbed my car keys and left.

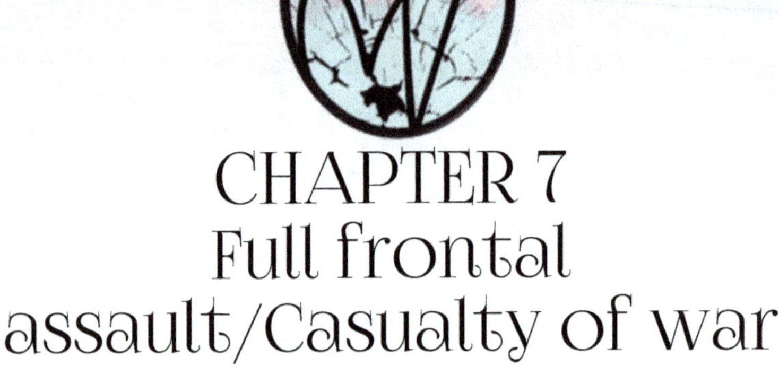

CHAPTER 7
Full frontal assault/Casualty of war

I wish I could say that I was able to drive off into the sunset and leave this murky part of my life behind. The reality is that this wasn't even the worst time of my life.

Pregnancy should be a wonderful time for couples to share the excitement of a new life, the different stages of growth, the cravings, mood swings, swollen feet and hot flashes. My pregnancy could not be further from this. At age 25, I was more than ready to be a mum.

When I said before that evil attempted everything in his power to crush and destroy me. I wasn't joking.

My pregnancy went something like this. This is not the exact chronological order, as my memories of this period are thwarted by trauma, so please excuse me if I am not entirely clear with the series of crazy events.

After deciding not to return home, to save this little baby growing inside me, I survived by sleeping in my car, on the sofas and floors of friends' houses, and had access to only a small amount of cash.

Looking back, I can still remember the desperation to be safe and free which overwhelmed me.

I quickly made my way to the council to register as homeless, in the hope of getting a place to stay pretty quickly. On this I was entirely wrong. Apparently, if you voluntarily leave your abode, you have made yourself intentionally homeless, and are not eligible to receive any financial or housing support of any kind. Domestic abuse was not considered a reason, and my pregnancy was still very early, so it could not be considered as a factor.

Emotionally wrecked from the sudden loss of my home, marriage, and life (friends and family), and being thrust into this weird faux poverty, while in the early stages of pregnancy, devastated my mental health.

I am ashamed to say, at that stage, I was certainly using drugs to numb the pain. I was trying so desperately to save my baby, but it seemed no one was coming to save me.

After several weeks, I re-established contact with Daemon to collect some clothing and other personal items. It took every ounce of emotional strength to do this. The few friends I had made contact with, either didn't want to get involved so would not speak to me, or had been told whatever lies Daemon had come up with this time and refused to talk to me.

Every route that may have resulted in me getting help throughout this time was strategically cut off, out of spite. Forcing me to go back to the only other place I could get help, which was Daemon.

In the end, that's exactly what happened, and I had to begrudgingly get in touch so I could get my ID documents, access to my money, clothing and any other personal items. After getting the grilling of a lifetime, Daemon used all his power to put me in a position where I would still have to give him some control over my life, if I wanted help.

He seemed to think my being pregnant gave him rights over my person, that the boy in my belly was his and I had no right to prevent him from doing whatever he wanted for his son.

It sounds so reasonable. That's the thing with Daemon, he made even the most ludicrous things sound plausible and the right thing to do. I didn't know it then, but he was a master manipulator, and I had been caught, hook, line and sinker.

In my weakness and desperation, I was persuaded to allow him to rent me a flat close by, so I could still have my independence, but he would be close enough to help out during the pregnancy. It seemed like a simple enough plan. I had no idea what this would eventually cost me. I had no other option, so agreed, and he rented a flat for me, paid the deposit, first month's rent and allowed me to take items from our (once) shared home to furnish the new place.

Just so you have an idea how close we lived to each other, I could see his flat from my living room window. This does not seem important at the moment, but there is a reason I mention it.

Despite all this crazy and emotional drama, I still had to look for a job because of my 'intentionally homeless' nonsense, and I really could not face having to rely on Daemon financially. That is one thing I was certain of.

Daemon had graciously reconnected my mobile phone (yet another thing he used to control me), so we were in regular contact again. The combination of the flat and mobile phone did something crazy to my husband. His need to control every element of my life kicked into overdrive, in a way I had never seen before.

Anytime I left or arrived at my flat, Daemon would be on the phone in seconds. I would often ignore him, as I just didn't want to have to deal with him. But he would call repeatedly without mercy until I answered. The call would then turn into a barrage of insults, abuse and threats, which were all spurred on by his own insecurities and character flaws.

Accusations of having men over, the baby not being his, rumours from this and that person drove him to 'crazy stalker' levels of madness, which would frequently devolve into trying to break into my flat, beating the doors and windows and making enough hullabaloo that neighbours would call the police.

I started to dread going back to the flat and would stay out at a friend's, occupying their floor or sofa for as many nights as they would allow me, so I didn't have to go home to face his constant harassment. That's not to say staying away solved the problem, because it didn't. I was receiving up to fifty telephone calls a day from him. Yes, you read right – 50 calls a day. It got so bad that my message box was so full, the phone operator would not allow any more messages to be stored.

Drunken, abusive, venomous ranting and accusations poured out of him like water over the falls. It was unrelenting, powerful, and destructive in a way that I don't have the capacity to express adequately. Let's just say that taking my own life crossed my mind more than once. I knew it would be less painful than this trauma-torment I was stuck in. The only thing that stopped me going through with it was baby Reece. We had never even met, but I knew he would be my saving grace in this whole sorry episode.

It is this notion of being torn between life and death that kept me in a precarious situation with Daemon for so long. He was always able to give me the financial and social stability I was never able to get by myself (I didn't even know it was an option back in those days). He was always willing to offer these things in return for my compliance.

Transactional relationships are not uncommon, and they take many forms. However, what usually happens is that both parties receive something they want from the other party as part of the exchange. What I had not realised was that the price was too high. This relationship was costing me things I had never considered important before, like my freedom to choose and make decisions for myself. Daemon had taken all those choices from me and replaced them with his choices. I felt like a puppet in the worst puppet show on earth. The audience couldn't see the strings, but I knew I was tethered to a master who seemed to give me life.

I eventually got a job at my local college, which at least gave me some income again, releasing me from the power of Daemon's money. At least for a little while, anyway.

I was four months pregnant and starting to show. I don't remember much about that time, but what I do remember was the disastrous holiday we went on. Daemon seemed to have accepted that we were no longer an item and suggested that we still go on a previously booked holiday. Of course, I had my reservations, but who in their right mind turns down what is effectively a free holiday?

We decided to go, not as a couple, but just so we could both get away, relax, and remove some of the stress which had been eating away at us both. On paper, it seemed like an OK idea. We were both adults, understood our new relationship, and that it was silly to waste a holiday in Tenerife. I would also not have been able to fly for much longer, and holidays would not be on the table for a while after Reece was born.

It was a nightmare from start to finish. Clearly Daemon was intent on torturing me the entire time by talking about his new girlfriend, spending hours on the phone with her and even asking me to choose a perfume at the duty-free shop. I initially thought he was buying it for me, until he said that his new girl would love it. Seriously, who asks their four-month-pregnant wife to pick perfume for their girlfriend?

I was raging, he was scheming, and in between the bitterness and rage, he still had the audacity to try to have sex with me. After being rebuffed so many times, we simply lost it with each other, and the holiday ended with us both sustaining emotional and physical injuries. I had slashed him with broken glass after breaking a vase during an argument. I was sporting several burns after he held me down while I was sleeping and stubbed his cigarette out on my face. I can honestly say that shit doesn't heal easily.

This messed up drama continued when we got back, as I quickly discovered the venomous vixen, he was shagging, loved nothing better than joining in his sick games to torment the pregnant wife. Opening my living room curtains to see her full-frontal naked body standing on his bedroom window sill for me to see was a torment too many.

I stormed round, pushed my way upstairs and grabbed this chick by the hair (she did have lovely hair!) and beat the crap out of her until Daemon managed to separate us. He claimed to not know she was doing this and asked her to leave.

I didn't believe that for a second. Now he made himself look like the hero by coming to my defence against the bad lady hurting my feelings. It was sick on so many levels, and I knew it was yet another ploy to get me to go back to him.

When trying to make me jealous didn't work, things got even more bizarre. One afternoon, as I was leaving my friend's house, I spotted an Asian man taking photographs of my car. I was a bit stunned and was about to ask what he was doing, when he turned the camera on me and started snapping away. He didn't seem to care he was being a blatant creep, and I drove away not really knowing what had happened.

Phone calls from Daemon were out of control. Multiple times a day he would call demanding to know where I was, who I was with, why I was at this or that place, why I hadn't answered his previous calls, why was I lying to him, who was the man I was seen with? Blah, blah, blah, etc.

The crazy thing is, when I answered, he didn't really want me to answer his questions. He just talked, ranted and raved and expected me to listen. Any response from me only made things worse, and the verbal abuse would come raining down like hot lava from an exploding volcano.

He threatened to stop paying the rent at least weekly, and I was calling the police with around the same frequency at this point, as his violent and crazy outbursts and attacks got more fiery and frequent.

We were entering 'crazy fan' territory.

I was summoned to the house (by a threat of not paying the rent) to be dressed down for my choice of friends. It was only then that I realised not only the lengths he would go to keep me captive, but he also had access to resources I never thought were available to regular humans like me and you.

I was presented with criminal record sheets of several people I knew and hung out with. Aside from being completely illegal, I was becoming increasingly scared of what else he was capable of. This is when he also told me about the private detective he had hired, and showed pictures of me with several people I knew and my car. This explained the weird Asian man taking my picture.

On more than one occasion, I got home to find all my kitchenware, electrical appliances and bedding gone. Daemon had broken in and taken everything I would need to keep me comfortable, in a ruse to get me to go back home.

On another occasion, I stayed over at a friend's house, but needed to go home in the morning to get ready for work. When I got home, I found Daemon naked and asleep in my bed. I was horrified and threw him out (yes, naked) before he was awake enough to realise what was happening. A passing bus full of commuters probably got more than they bargained for that morning.

He had found out about my new job (probably from the private detective), and I was now subjected to almost daily harassment. He would be waiting in the car park at work when my shift finished. He was also harassing staff members at the college, pressing them for information about me, and making himself a massive pain in the ass and a liability to my job.

This eventually came to a head when a complaint was made against me. The receptionist in the department where I work was being harassed by Daemon in person and via the phone, pushing the poor lady to tears, with her refusing to come back unless the situation was dealt with.

After a very long one-to-one with my manager, I was lucky not to be sacked. This was definitely how she felt (although she was never crazy about me in the first place), and I left with a warning that any more incidents would result in a formal grievance against me.

Just what I needed; six months pregnant, a victim of domestic abuse and harassment, and my employer choosing to punish me for a situation I had no control over. Some days, being a black woman is worse than others. That day was a perfect example of double discrimination. I doubt that if a white woman had disclosed to her boss that she was subject to domestic abuse and ongoing harassment she would have left with an informal warning. Support services would have been rushed in, there would have been paid leave, special circumstances and access to occupational therapy services.

Why wasn't I treated like a victim? I hear you ask. Simple. If you are black, it's always your fault. Even if those words are never said out loud, the resulting actions always expose the reality of people's bias. If my boss saw me as a victim, I would have been treated like a victim. The fact is, even after I told her what I have told you, I was treated like the perpetrator and threatened with disciplinary action.

There is nothing to appropriately describe the experience of society rubbing salt into your wounds, for no other reason than you fit their biased stereotype. This is something that would come to bite me in the ass, time and time again.

Daemon was by now a beast who was stalking, harassing, abusing, and destroying me day by day. I had no power to stop or prevent it and no one came to my aid or defence. Up to then, the police had been nothing more than a way to record 'alleged incidents,' as told by my husband.

Thankfully, one night changed everything. I still can't really tell if it was for the better, but it at least gave me a shot at freedom.

On a particularly bad night of repeated phone calls, I had decided to ignore him no matter how many times he phoned, knocked on the door or banged on the windows. I had taken to sitting in the dark, because every time I turned on the lights in my flat, it would provoke another flurry of vicious phone calls. It was times like this that helped me to become bedfellows with both fear and darkness.

Had I known then that this was the doorway to my darkness, I may have made different choices.

In a drunken rage, Daemon had started hammering on my flat doors and windows, trying to get me to respond to his phone calls. I refused to engage with him, and eventually went to bed, in the dark, listening to his verbal abuse and battery of my abode. I let that darkness try to hide me; it was like a surreal protection from the evil he took everywhere with him, and I thought it would keep me safe long enough for him to get fed up and go home.

Instead, the darkness was broken by the shattering of glass, which poured, sprinkled and scratched my face and arms as I lay there in my bed. I don't think Daemon ever intended to do that, because he promptly ran off, leaving me covered in shards of glass in the dark, and wind blowing through my bedroom through the hole where the window used to be.

I managed to dial the police who, for a change, did not take too long to arrive. My name was already familiar to them and had been flagged for previous domestic violence incidents. For once, the police were quick to respond to me as a victim, and immediately asked if I had somewhere else to stay.

I did not, so they told me to pack what I could, as they no longer felt it was safe for me to remain in the property. I knew they had only done this because of Reece. My belly was swollen, despite my thin facial features and bony limbs. They knew I was pregnant and, statistically, pregnant women in domestic violence situations have very poor outcomes. Their unborn babies have even worse outcomes. That night, Reece saved my life. For once, I was seen as a vulnerable victim, and the system finally got to work in my favour. I was taken to a nearby hostel while I waited to be rehoused.

CHAPTER 8
War zone

After being removed from my home for my own safety, I ended up in a hostel. The hostel was crazy. Firstly, it was in the middle of nowhere. I actually would not be able to find it again, if asked. It was walled, with razor wire on the outer walls, a video doorbell system and reception area where visitors are kept separate from residents. It was pretty big; four floors with at least ten rooms per floor. There were families of all shapes and sizes there. There were a few pregnant women like me but also couples and many families with multiple children, often having to split between two to three rooms.

Kitchens and bathrooms were shared (aside from a few ensuites). This meant queues, stolen toiletries, fighting for cooker space, kitchenware, and privacy. I refused to complain about this safe haven. Despite its less-than-luxury status, it provided safety for me and other mothers and families from across our region. The staff were vigilant in maintaining security; no one who didn't live there could gain entry without a pre-approved invitation.

Siblings would play in the corridors because there was no outdoor space. No one really had a TV unless they brought their own (which was rare when you are escaping domestic abuse). The TV lounge was like a doctor's waiting room: cold, full of leaflets and dull like a crinkled old newspaper.

I remember there being a lot of noise: traffic from a nearby main road, crying, shouting, running, random alarms from who knows where. All the noise was suffocating, yet completely isolating. I knew no one. I had no one to tell where I was. I was living in this weird space which wasn't quite death or hell but wasn't quite a sanctuary either. It's what I imagine purgatory would be like.

In less than a week, I was told I would have to be moved to another facility. It seems my being pregnant brought limited support. Families with children were the priority for this centre and, as I did not yet have a child, I was considered less vulnerable and could be moved to another property.

Over the next couple of months, I was moved to around five different hostels, homes and halfway houses, never staying longer than a week or two and always waiting to be moved on.

My work had all but fizzled out. My boss had decided to reduce my hours to the point it wasn't worth me staying on. I knew it was by design, but I simply did not have the energy to fight it, and maybe not being at work was exactly what I needed. My mental health was deteriorating quickly, and I was struggling to eat (which is vital in pregnancy) and was still occasionally smoking cigarettes, crack and weed whenever I felt overwhelmed.

I don't recall attending any ante-natal classes, and I am pretty sure I missed my second scan. With the frequent moves and being unable to keep medical services updated, I simply fell through the cracks. Reece seemed well as far as I could tell, and I would spend long nights unable to sleep, just rubbing my belly, talking to him and watching as his little limbs formed lumps and bumps on my ever-expanding body.

To compound the situation, my car was broken into while I was at work. There was no evidence tying it to Daemon, but at that point, I certainly wouldn't have put it past him. With all my other worries, it seemed like a small thing. I called the insurance company to make a claim, only to find out that my insurance was invalid, as Daemon had stopped paying the car insurance three months before and hadn't bothered to inform me.

I don't know why I was even surprised. This man did everything in his power to remove any support, destroy my ability to earn an income, force me out of the home he had helped me to get, and harassed me to the point I wanted to kill myself. Why stop there! Now I was unable to claim any money to repair my car, and I felt like the entire world was against me.

I know this probably wasn't true, but your mind plays tricks on you when you are forced into situations that cause you harm, and especially when there seems to be no way out. I started to wonder if I had committed some heinous sin that required the strictest kind of punishment.

I had committed lots of sins. I still was committing them; I had gone my own way, ignored God's path and the wisdom of people around me. Maybe this was why everything I touched turned to shit?

This frame of mind allowed me to put myself into extremely vulnerable situations and, twice during my pregnancy, I had my bank card stolen (by people I knew) and had my bank account emptied.

These were the kinds of people I was hanging around with: addicts, thieves, working girls, dealers and general low lives. I felt that, somehow, I was just like them, so I gravitated to spending time with people I knew didn't care about me and would not think twice about using me to gain something for themselves.

Weirdly, I felt safer around those sorts of people than opening myself up to Daemon. With them, I knew exactly what I was getting and the risks I was taking. Daemon felt like a sick joke. A twisted prank gone wrong or a punishment from God for committing the worst crimes imaginable. It makes me sad to think of this now, and I wonder how many other people out there are trapped by their own lack of self-worth, lack of value and have exposed themselves to harm because they think that's all they are worth?

If it makes me sad, it definitely makes God sad.

After many months apart, I finally reconnected with my sister Serena, who let me stay over from time to time. It was so good being in an environment that was not cold and sterile. Serena is like part of my flesh. We were born two years apart but somehow she always knew what I was thinking or feeling and vice versa. It's what I imagine twins experience.

I know it was hard for Serena during this time. I would change my mind at a moment's notice, fly off the handle over little things and eat everything I could see. I would spend many hours awake (disturbing everyone at night) or many hours sleeping and basically ignoring the world around me. I guess that's how I coped with the emotional toll this season had imposed upon me.

Serena even tolerated the harassment, abusive phone calls and ranting from both me and Daemon. She never lost her temper, asked anything of me, or expected anything. She was the one person in the world I knew I could call on, day or night.

I was still effectively estranged from my parents and younger brother, but I had no idea how to bridge that gap. "Hi mum. Sorry I haven't been in touch for 18 months. Oh, and by the way, I am pregnant, homeless and escaping domestic violence." This is not a conversation anyone wants to have on a good day, let alone on a bad day.

I had so much guilt and shame for the situation I found myself in. It was these feelings that kept me from attempting to restore my familial relationships. At least in part. It was only a strange twist of fate that eventually restored our connection.

I was well into trimester three of my pregnancy and still living and moving around from hostel to hostel. I was about eight months pregnant, tired, emotional and without significant support. I had decided to go for a walk to try to escape the madness of staring at the four walls of my room. This particular hostel was noisy, tense and unfriendly.

During my walk, I noticed I was really struggling to walk at any kind of normal pace. This is not unusual for a pregnant woman. However, I began to experience excruciating pain in my hips and back and ended up collapsing on the street. I couldn't get to my feet and just lay there in a heap, wiggling around and trying to move.

From the ground, I could see a police car on the other side of the street. The two officers had pulled over a red car and were interrogating the three occupants. I wondered why they hadn't come over to help me, or in fact noticed the heavily pregnant black woman lying on the floor? Thankfully, a local resident had seen my collapse and came out to help me back to the hostel. An ambulance was immediately called, and I was taken to the hospital.

I lost the next few days doped up on opiates in the hospital. When I came to, I felt cold and sick. One would assume it was the medication or cool temperatures in the hospital, but it was not that kind of cold and sick. As I came around, sitting in a chair next to my bed was Daemon, reading the paper as if nothing was wrong. For a few minutes, I simply didn't know how to respond. I was like a deer frozen in shiny headlights on a country road.

My head was spinning, my stomach churned as I reeled with the shock of seeing Daemon sitting next to me. I closed my eyes and pretended to go back to sleep. I listened to the busy sounds of the hospital ward to distract me. Daemon was laughing and joking with the nurses, flirting and making everyone laugh.

How dare he! After terrorising me for years, causing me to become homeless while pregnant, almost killing our baby before he drew a breath and doing everything in his power to destroy me.He sat there laughing and acting like he was king of the castle.

I couldn't work out how he had found me, but I soon learned that Daemon was still listed as my next of kin in my hospital records. My only saving grace was my emergency contacts also included my little sister Serena, who in turn contacted my parents. It was a strange time, and I don't really remember how I felt about everything. I was pregnant, in pain, still homeless and trying to make sense of what the hell my life looked like now.

Over the next six weeks, things really started to turn around and, for the first time in a long time, I began to think about God again. Despite all the craziness of my life, I was reconnected with my family, and I finally started to feel like I belonged again. It was weird, but my parents really made an effort to include me and consider me.

I soon got a house to live in, right around the corner from my sister, and although it was completely unfurnished with concrete floors, no curtains, cooker, bed or anything at all, it was mine. I had two sofa chairs donated by my sister's friends and a little portable TV. At night, I would turn the two chairs to face each other as a makeshift bed. I didn't care. I finally felt some safety, some shelter, in my little hideaway from Daemon and the world. I could make a new start with my baby boy, who would be along very soon.

This was the first time I had felt any excitement about the new life I was carrying, and I was quietly grateful to God that we had both made it this far. Things could only get better.

There must have been something of immense value inside me or planned for me, for the enemy to go to such lengths to destroy me. There are still parts of that time that I have not opened up about and, honestly, I don't feel that I need to anymore. I don't tell you these things to gain your sympathy. I just wanted you to know that I can now look back on what was going on during this period in my life having to come to terms with how I was treated by my ex. Understanding it in terms of my purpose has certainly made it easier to accept, forgive and move on with God.

CHAPTER 9
First responder

I am sorry to keep offloading on you, but I feel it's important to tell my story in full. I never really appreciated, until recently, how much I don't talk. Not in the general way that people chit-chat with neighbours, but choosing to delve into pain and trauma to help the healing process, allowing God's Holy Spirit to heal those deep and broken parts.

Unless you have walked in the shoes of people like me and the other victims of abuse and addicts, it's very hard to explain to people the level of loneliness, isolation, and abandonment many of us have been through.

It wasn't just a passing phase for many of us; it's a place where we lived and breathed, day in and day out. We became one with the pain, and the emptiness, with a hole in our life that should have been filled with people you love and who love you back. But instead of those loving and fulfilling relationships, the space was filled with fear and hate which we tried to numb with substances. Addictions look selfish and they are, but the reality is that survival is selfish. Every victim of abuse and every addict is battling for their own survival and simply don't have the capacity to make selfless decisions. This is what trauma looks like. At first you fight against it, trying to convince yourself that you are not a victim and you are not like other addicts. You profess to have more going for you and have total control of your life. But the day comes to us all, when we realise, we have been living in the darkness so long that we don't know any other way to live.

That's what I felt like before going to Victory House. I was separated from everything and everyone I knew and loved. I felt a hollow aching. I was alone and knew I had to fight a battle to get beyond my feelings. That's something that no one ever talks about. You hear the compliments of bravery for taking that step to get clean from drugs, crime, and trauma. What people don't know is that it's not bravery that drives people like me to places like Victory House; it's the complete opposite. We are driven by desperation, fear, loneliness and a nagging feeling that, without help, we simply won't make it.

In fairness, even with help, some of us still don't make it. I have lost count of the women and girls who were supported to transform their lives, only to be drawn back to the only thing they knew. The potential of a new life slipped through their hands like sand because they were too afraid to change or they didn't have the right support to rebuild their life. Changing your life is an impossible task. We attempt to rely on our willpower, resilience, and determination to change our lives. The reality is that we have all walked through the crucible of flames but not everyone makes it out unscathed.

The crucible of flames is the ultimate test in life. Like an inverted mountain that holds the fire from the centre of the earth. Instead of snowy peaks with brave men attempting to prove their metal on treacherous climbs. there are people like me, trying not to be sucked into the fiery lava, while clutching and grasping the ever-increasing incline below our feet. Here we don't suffer from frostbite or snowstorms. Instead, everything we touch burns through our flesh and the storms are made from sulphur and ash. The more you try to steady yourself, the more injuries you incur. Your eyes are blinded by ash, your nose and mouth blister from the sulphur fumes, and you realise that you can never escape without help.

Victory House was like a St Bernard you send to rescue mountain climbers. You lead a team of rescuers to the injured party bringing first aid, protective equipment and something to nourish the thirsty dying soul in front of them. We know that without your intervention, the likelihood of our survival is miniscule and even with help, not everyone who is rescued survives. Those who have experienced support and love are overjoyed to be rescued. However, for those who have been abused, abandoned and harmed, there is nothing that describes the fear of feeling that no one is coming to save you. This is exactly where I was when God stepped into my life.

Trust was one of my main challenges as I journeyed through my recovery. Mine and Serena's dad had walked out on our mum when I was about five (making Serena three years old). I know it's not a unique situation, and countless people have grown up in similar circumstances. However, the pain that stems from that type of abandonment runs deep. When you compound that with a strained parental relationship (my mum and stepdad Richard), which resulted in me leaving home at the age of 15 and being estranged from them for the next three years, the scars grow a little deeper. Combine that with a nomadic childhood moving from house to house, town to town, city to city and never feeling like you had a place to call home; never staying long enough to establish friendship groups, and the few friends you had were dropped as soon as the next house move was announced.

My first break-up (after seven great years) left me wondering why life was so full of disappointment and why no one valued me? Then came Daemon who, rather than love me, treated me like property he owned, taking what little self-esteem, power and self-worth I had managed to retain, after life had systematically robbed me.

It is from this position I was expected to conquer the crucible.

I always imagine this is the part where God steps in, kills the flames with his living water and lets his broken child walk right through the crucible, unscathed.

Well, God most certainly stepped in, but it was not at all in the way I expected.

Memories are such funny things. I can still hear the soft tones of my counsellor's voice and remember the dust particles billowing through the sun streaming through the attic office. The slanted roof and small window that didn't look like it offered much light, but some days, if you caught the right hour of the day, golden rays of sunshine would pour through the net curtains.

It was these sorts of memories that took me back to one of the oddest experiences of my life. I know I briefly mentioned that I came back to God after an unusual experience. I don't tell many people as even to me, it sounds a bit crazy. But every word is true, and the experience changed my life forever.

When Reece was less than a year old, we went on holiday to Florida for a family celebration. Looking back, it was definitely a God-plan, as I was a broke, single mum trying to kick a drug habit and still fighting the curse of my ex. I had been diagnosed with postnatal depression, and God knew I needed a holiday.

I should have already twigged that something interesting was going to happen when a lady from my parents' church phoned to give me a message. She explained that she had intended to go to Florida with my parents and other family members. She had paid for her flights and accommodation and was excited to spend some time exploring the USA and meeting our family. However, she believed that God had told her to let me go in her place, and she was transferring the flight and accommodation bookings into my name.

I really didn't know what to say. No one had ever given me a holiday like this before and it wasn't like Daemon, who loved to flash his cash and make a big event of gifts so that people would think he was generous and kind. This was entirely different. I knew this lady, but not well. We hadn't talked much before, so she had no reason to consider giving me her tickets. What kind of person does that?

After eventually realising she was being serious and having a few more conversations to pass on information, I was booked on a holiday to Florida with my baby boy. It was strange spending time with my parents and family after so long without them in my life. I didn't hate it, and everyone was sure not to bring up anything uncomfortable for the whole trip.

It was great to get away from the daily stresses of living under constant threat. I was a new mum fighting a drug addiction and an ex-husband. I was weary, bruised and felt like I had failed. However, while out for a walk with a few family members, I was lost in my own thoughts, when God abruptly interrupted me.

I was pushing Reece in his buggy down a residential street, the sun was blazing, and I was enjoying the quiet roads (Floridians don't walk in the heat). As I walked and looked around, I almost bumped the buggy into something metal. As I got my bearings, I realised it was a ladder. I know that doesn't sound very strange, but it was.

Houses in this area were set way back from the pavement, at least six to eight metres, which was covered in the richest, greenest lawns you have ever seen. This ladder was directly in the middle of the pavement. It stood completely upright, with one end on the ground and the other end shot straight up into the sky.

I took a few steps back to try to work out how this was possible. This was not an A-frame ladder, yet it was free-standing on one end, with nothing in the vicinity to support or balance it. It was just there, an oddity in the middle of the path, towering up into the sky. It was so long, I could not see the top of the ladder at all, as it went straight up into the sky and eventually disappeared into a cloud.

Looking back, I should have been way more freaked out, but instead, I was more puzzled than anything else. As I squinted to get a clearer look at what was unfolding before me, I noticed that there were people on the ladder. Some were climbing quickly as if there was some sort of race, standing and clambering over slower or stationary people so they could overtake them.

Others were climbing one-handed because they were carrying bags or sacks. Some were overloaded with several bags in one hand as well as a backpack, others had only a briefcase, and some had no baggage at all. Some must have had considerable weight in their bags because they were struggling to climb under the weight of their sacks, and periodically lost their grip, slipping down several rungs as people climbed and scrambled over them.

I even noticed a few people carrying bags in their teeth, wearing office shoes, skirts, and trouser suits, which were wholly inappropriate attire for the task. It looked dangerous, and I sharply inhaled as a few precarious bodies looked as if they might slip right off and fall to their deaths.

Eventually my worst fears were realised and, one by one, people slipped, lost their grip or footing and fell from a great height. I desperately wanted to turn away and run in case bodies started to fall on me, but I couldn't move. In fact, I don't think I was even standing on the ground anymore? My perspective of the ladder had been altered while I inspected the details, and I was somehow elevated, and able to see much more than previously.

The horror of watching these poor people fall to their deaths was shocking and, to make matters worse, not a single person on the ladder reached out to help anyone else. They didn't even seem shocked at watching people fall or take notice of what was happening. There was just this dark drive to get to the top of this mystery ladder at any cost. For some the cost was very high, and they lost their lives in pursuit of whatever they were so desperate to grasp.

Every time someone fell from the ladder, I was expecting a sea of eyes to follow them down as they plummeted. Instead, those remaining on the ladder continued to look up and power on toward whatever was at the other end. I looked up and tried to catch a glimpse of what everyone was chasing, but I could see nothing. As the ladder stretched high, its upper sections were clouded with a thick fog which prevented anyone from seeing what was at the other end. These people must be crazy! They were risking life and limb to get to the top of the mystery ladder, and they had no idea what was at the top. Despite this obvious flaw in their thinking, people continued their treacherous journey to the unknown.

I blinked and was suddenly in a different place. The scene was a woodland path, which was wide enough for only one person to walk at a time. I looked down (I was still in this weird elevated position) and I saw the figure of a person, walking along a path with woodland-type countryside all around. It was full of trees, bushes and long grasses. Directly ahead but further away was a clear white light. Despite it being the middle of the day, the light still lit up the path, and the person seemed to be heading in the direction of this little light.

There were bushes and branches growing along the side of the path. He stepped unsteadily, either to avoid the overgrowth, or as if not quite sure where he was going. I continued to watch with interest, noticing that the brambles and bushes had started to breach the path, making it almost impassable. As he walked, I could see him faltering as he tripped on brambles, which left cuts and scratches on his lower legs.

He had clearly had enough and decided to look for an alternative path. To the left of the path, it looked like the brambles started to clear, and the ground became softer. There were fewer brambles and bushes, and it wasn't far from the path, so he took the detour. After walking a short time, he realised his eyes had been deceived, as the path once again grew hard and stony, causing him to stumble onto thorny brambles which caused him to bleed through his clothing. He continued, hoping the area would clear soon but instead, the trees, foliage and brambles became thicker, and the trees grew close together overhead, causing long shadows to form across the terrain.

The light was all but blotted out by the towering trees, and I could feel unrest and trepidation as walking became fumbling and seeing became blindness in the unknown darkness.

By now he was lost and panicking, and I found myself shallow breathing as I looked on, feeling helpless. He would not give in, and aimlessly stumbled around for what felt like hours. He was clearly tired, sore and covered in bloody patches from bleeding wounds concealed underneath (what was now) soiled and torn clothing. Exhausted and sorrowful, he finally stood still, as if to try to get his bearings. He looked up and, as if out of nowhere, light was suddenly shining all around.

I could feel the intense relief and delight as he realised he was saved by this light. A rush of hope surged through my body as I watched him follow the light and carefully amble through the woodland toward the light. The light was closer, and I could see it was only a small floating lantern. The light it shed enabled him to carefully tread around rocks, avoid being caught up in the brambles, and progress became quicker.

Every now and again he tried to look around to see further into the darkness, but each time he instantly became entangled in brambles, tripped and fell to the ground. Each time he stood up, brushed himself down, wiped his scratches and continued to walk ahead while refocusing on the lamp. It was obvious that the way through this was to keep his eyes on the light.

After walking a while, he came upon a giant obstacle in the path. A very large tree had fallen across it, and much foliage, plants and other life was growing on it, so it must have been there for some time. This giant tree trunk which lay across the path was covered in vines that crept along the ground and all around the trunk. This had paved the way for surrounding plant life and the roots of neighbouring trees and bushes to become entangled. Together, they created a criss-cross network which resembled lattice or gauze.

He had already experienced trying to take a shortcut and had no desire to repeat that process. The only choice was to go straight through the obstacle, slowly and carefully. Up until then, the light had stayed steadily in front, guiding him forward, as long as he continued looking at it. Now he had to focus his attention to the knotted ground beneath his feet, step by step; carefully and always trying to assess his next step, making his way very slowly. It seemed like the ground was getting even thicker with undergrowth.

Suddenly, he tripped, fell and landed in the undergrowth. He tried to get back up but soon realised his feet were tangled in the criss-cross of vines that layered the ground. He began to panic and look around him, but it immediately started getting dark again. He remembered what he did last time he was in trouble. I watched as he closed his eyes, and I instinctively knew what he was doing. He was remembering the light and as the thought came into his mind, as if by will alone, the light appeared, the vines began to fall away, and he was released. He stood up and confidently walked towards the light, never taking his eyes off it. Before he realised it, he was back on the path, which had become clear again.

I heard a gentle but very clear voice. Looking back, I should have been shocked or scared but, somehow, I wasn't. It felt as if everything I was seeing and hearing was completely normal, and it did not concern me in the slightest. The voice said, "I am the light that will guide your footsteps." Without any words being exchanged, I knew that all I had to do was follow the light. I knew it would protect me from the snares and traps along my life journey, and that challenges would be a regular occurrence, as I followed the light of God. I was reminded that this was God's way and, although there were many dangers, God would always protect me, if I had faith to follow the light.

I suddenly heard my name being called: "Donna ... Donna." It grew louder and I was conscious that I needed to pay attention. It seemed as if I blinked and instantly found myself standing on the pavement in the blistering Floridian sun. My family were about one hundred metres down the road, and I could see someone frantically waving and shouting my name and urging me to hurry up.

I quickly grabbed the buggy handles, checked Reece was OK and gently jogged so I could catch up with them all. I wasn't sure what I had experienced but I knew it was important and that I needed time to think.

CHAPTER 10
The gardener and the thorns

I have been reminiscing over my time at Victory House and how much it laid the foundations for my future. The daily church and bible studies were my favourite part of the day. I honestly don't know why, because most people felt it was torture and didn't see why this was needed every day.

What the residents didn't realise is that we were being prepared with good habits of seeking God daily, making time for Him before anything else and learning to listen to the Holy Spirit.

This is something that I have kept with me all these years. Don't get me wrong, I have seasons of not reading my bible, or missing church more than usual and not giving God the first part of my day. But I do commune with Him daily in lots of small, less formal ways that keep me connected and in tune with Him. One of my favourite ways is with manual tasks. We had plenty of those at Victory House, including cooking, cleaning, gardening, or sorting clothes in the donation shed. They knew how to keep us occupied.

I don't really know what the purpose behind this daily manual work was but, for me, it opened a world I never knew existed. I learned to hear God in the small things, in the mundane, the daily grind that brought me untold joy and closeness. I had literally never experienced a relationship like this, and I loved every minute. To people looking in, it looked like I was ignoring the world, unsociable, and a loner. The truth is, I had learned to find my way to God amid the hustle and bustle of everyday life.

This is the thing that has never left me. Let me give you one of my favourite examples.

At the time, Victory House seemed like a labour camp most days, but the surroundings were breathtakingly beautiful. For the first time ever, I was allowed out of the main complex to do some gardening work in one of the cottage properties owned by the rehab. It was stunning, and I was even more thrilled when I was asked to do a job all by myself. Hallelujah.

I didn't have to tolerate the moaning and bitching of that motley crew of recovering addicts. It was just me and God in the sunshine. The air was fragrant and warm as I stood outside in the garden. I looked around and could see God's handiwork looking back at me in every direction. To one side of the garden lay a dense tangle of a bush, thick with thorns and foliage, almost strangling itself with a deep complex network of roots, branches and weeds that seemed to spread from every direction.

My job that day was to cut this bad boy down. I stood close and it was easily six or seven feet tall and as wide as a small van. Somewhere in this devastation was a live and beautiful bush. All I had to do was free it. It was at that moment, God showed me something amazing.

The bush was once healthy and alive, but its life had been almost strangled out of existence. It was penetrated on all sides by giant thorns, weeds and thistles which encroached and suffocated it. It couldn't grow, couldn't see the light and, without care and attention from a gardener, it would certainly die.

That day, God showed me the nature of a true gardener. I didn't even need to close my eyes; somehow, God was able to show me things while I was wide awake, allowing me to see things other people can't. I don't know how he does it or why, but I have grown to love this secret part of my life with God.

I watched as the gardener arrived, looking over the mangled mess of the bush and beginning to examine it carefully. Instead of getting an axe to start chopping it down (which would have been a simple option for most), he picked up a small set of pruners. He began to very carefully snip and clip the weeds and drop them to the ground where they could do no harm.

He was careful to protect the bush hidden inside this tangled mess. Whenever he spotted green foliage belonging to the bush, he tenderly caressed the leaves and trimmed away the weeds and dross surrounding it so one more part was freed. He worked at this for a very long time, never getting impatient or willing to lose a live part to get the job done quicker. He painstakingly cut and snipped away at the mass only when it was safe to do so without damaging the bush contained within.

His hand was always gentle and considerate, giving the greatest care to protect what was his. I looked down at his hands and noticed they were shredded and bleeding from being ripped at by the giant thorns. I don't remember seeing him wince in pain, not even once. I imagined the pain he must feel being pricked and torn by the thorny overgrown mass he was attempting to tame.

My memory was suddenly pricked. There was another who bled for me. He too knew the searing pain of thorns being driven into flesh. The thorns were made into a crown of mockery and driven deep into his skull. My Jesus, the pain and suffering you must have endured on the cross is something I can only imagine in the feeblest terms. My eyes were starting to burn, and a hot, solitary tear escaped my eye and began to roll down my cheek.

The gardener continued working tirelessly, cutting back and destroying everything that was broken, withered or ugly, and destroying them. There were even a few parts of the bush that were so devastated they could not be saved, so the gardener cut them off and threw them to the ground with the other weeds and thorns. I knew this wasn't done out of malice or lack of care. He was making room for something new to grow, which could never happen if the space was being occupied by something which was dead, dying, or killing off other healthy parts of the bush.

Eventually, he reached the very heart of the bush.

After cutting back all the death and decay, something was being revealed. The last of the thorns had enveloped this precious thing at the centre of the bush. I had to strain my neck to get a better look at what was hidden. To my surprise, completely hidden beneath this ugly mass was a nest, and, in it a single egg.

I could not believe that hidden underneath this ugly mass, a precious egg had been laid. In fact, the egg had been purposely placed in the nest, knowing it would be completely protected until its time. Even though surrounded by thorns and thistles, which were ugly and painful, they actually served to protect the precious life within. When the time was right, the egg would hatch and God would send little birds of faith and hope to feed, nurture and protect them. God always sends help when needed.

The egg had been planted in me many years before and laid in the nest of my heart, which would protect it against any enemy. God had cleared away the debris of my life so that the new life within me could be born and flourish. When mature, the young bird would be strong enough and eventually leave the dark confines of the bush and fly free, being carried through the air by the very breath of God, into its future.

This was what happened to my spirit. It had to be crushed and strangled almost out of existence. But God 'The Gardener' had a plan for me. Even before I knew, he had placed his life inside me. And when the time was right, he worked on me day and night to restore what had almost been destroyed. He sent me help, hope and faith to guide and nurture me. Eventually, his very breath caused my spirit to soar.

This inspiration impressed a truth into my heart, that this tangled mess is our lives, and God is our careful and loving gardener. Step by step, branch by branch and thorn by thorn, he will destroy our old and broken lives. What emerges will be astounding, amazing, beautiful, strong and capable. God will take us into our future by giving us new wings. We will be carried on the wind of his love, safely to our destiny.

That day, I started to know and understand the truth of God's love.

CHAPTER 11
The negotiation

It was good to visit the goodness of God and be reminded of why Victory House is such an important place for me, and many others like me.

After I came back from Florida, I was in a state of confusion about what to do for a month. It seems ridiculous looking back now, as anyone with an ounce of sense would have said, "Yes Lord." However, I thought it was time to negotiate terms with God.

I was one hundred percent sure that God spoke to me that day in Florida, but somehow, being back home, it felt even more real and even more important. Knowing that God had spoken to me without audible words was very odd. I had been raised on bible stories where God seemed to speak in audible words that came from the clouds. I distinctly remember Moses listening to God while the clouds parted, and sunrays shot down to the earth below. I know I heard him, and I knew what he wanted. I just couldn't figure out why?

The first part of my vision was the ladder. This ladder clearly represented the human version of success that eventually leads to nowhere, just like the ladder. It's the archetypal rat race where people accumulate wealth, status and power in a race to the top. It's worthless, and many lose their lives in its pursuit. The second part was journeying with God. Even though I may lose my way and wander, he will always find me. I may stumble, fall and be injured, but I will always be healed. I may come against things that will overpower me and block my path, but he will always rescue me. All I needed to do was call him. I don't know about you, but that didn't exactly sound like a good deal. Choosing between a rat race of death versus a traumatised traveller seemed like God was having a laugh.

I knew exactly what God wanted, and for some reason, it was me. I just didn't know if I wanted to give myself over to him. Life was not perfect (well, actually, far from perfect), but I was surviving and didn't believe God had the willingness or ability to change my life in the way I wanted. And from the looks of it, if I became that journeyman, it might not be any better. Why on earth would I sign up for that willingly?

It's funny looking back on these conversations. It's as if my mind had been poisoned by the things of the world and I actually began to bargain with God. I was determined that if God wanted me to give myself to him, then it was only fair that I got something in return. I am definitely embarrassed thinking about this now but at the time, I was deadly serious about the whole thing.

I am not even sure what I was asking for? An easier life maybe? One with less drama, fewer crazy exes, fewer people who wanted to take, take, take. That would have been a good start, I suppose. After several weeks trying to wrap my head around what my life might look like with God in the driving seat, I decided to take out the bible my mum bought me as a teenager, to try to get some answers. What I didn't expect (and was totally stunned by) was actually an answer.

I opened the bible and it fell open on Psalm 119 v 105:

"By your words I can see where I'm going; they throw a beam of light on my dark path" (MSG).

After reading this, I knew God's word had penetrated a long forgotten part of my heart. I needed more time to think about what I was going to do. The following weeks were a stressful and confusing time as I tried to negotiate my surrender with God. My experience had a profound impact on me, and I never really had a concept of success before. I have always done what is expected of me, until I couldn't do it any longer. I then swung in the complete opposite direction of expectations and lost myself in my attempt to get away from a life that felt dangerous and constricted. I know what other people considered as being 'successful,' and I knew I did not feel the same way.

I was not totally sure what I thought, but I knew for sure I did not value material possessions or wealth. I have never tried to get either, (and my family still call me a 'hippy' because of my low-maintenance lifestyle).

I sensed that God had already put a desire in me to be with Him and want Him. He would be the source of my success, he would be my light, if I was faithful and kept my eyes on Him. It's very humbling to realise God – the big guy who created everything – spoke directly to me. It wasn't a second-hand message, delivered by a spiritual do-gooder, or a random bible verse I could misinterpret.

I felt like my mind and spirit had a direct, two-way video link to God. It must have been what Saul felt like after his road to Damascus experience. Except Saul, being an obedient sort, immediately gave himself over to God. I, however, did not. After about a month of debating and discussing with God the terms and conditions of my salvation (or surrender!), I finally made my decision.

Unfortunately for me, I discovered the only terms and conditions I could use in this relationship all belonged to God, not me. And there ended my short career as a negotiator.

I will never forget that time. It marked a very clear turning point for me. I had two choices clearly outlined, and it felt like the most important decision I ever made. God showed me a vision of a man. He was alone walking along a path, and many times he went the wrong way, got lost and hurt, but every time this happened, he looked ahead and there was a light to guide him.

Every time the man looked away from the light, even when it was to look at whatever danger faced him, he was overcome, but when he lifted his head towards the light, the danger would pass him by, and he would be saved or restored to the right path.

As I look back at this vision, I remember understanding for the first time that everything I needed in my life was found in that light but, to accept it, I had to raise my head and look at it. I had to look to God. The action of the man raising his head seems so significant now.

In human society, to lower your head is to show respect to another person. Someone who walks with their head raised or held high is a sign they have respect for themselves. Having that relationship with God (with the light), I was forced to look up. He caused me to raise my head. A relationship with God causes us to respect ourselves; for our respect is not found in what we think of ourselves, or what we gain in this life, or what others think of us, but in what God believes of us.

For the first time, in a very long time, I felt hope for my future; a sense of purpose and a desire to get to know God for myself. That same night, I prayed a prayer, which I still have written in an old notebook, to remind me of my promise to God.

'My God, this is my promise to you.

I will seek you first before anything. I will show my love by my obedience to your word. I will not shy away from the difficult tasks you present to me. I will depend on you for all of this. I will continually search for your wisdom and understanding in all things. I will follow you to foreign lands and depend on you for all my provisions. Holy Spirit, you reside in me, take my heart for it belongs to you. I will love your children, as you love your children. I will spread your word as you have taught me, and I will depend on you always. Your kingdom will be my highest priority. Lord, I will be used by you because I am your willing servant. I will depend on you for all things.

Amen.'

Over the next few weeks and months, I was filled with a joy I had never known before. I felt closer to God than at any other time in my life, and I felt his presence with me daily. I had begun to sing and worship (which I had never done before) and started to really love the time I spent with God.

God continued to reveal himself to me through scripture, worship songs and the world around me. I had started going back to church with my parents and began to feel the rift between us healing. God seemed like he was keeping his promises to me.

I recall having another waking vision while at my parents' house. It was different to the last one as I could physically feel things, which hadn't happened before. I felt this really odd connection, like being dipped into a warm bath but on the inside of my body.

I was in the kitchen facing a cupboard (which is not unusual, as kitchens have cupboards). Everything else faded away and all I could see was a single cupboard; plain, made of wood with a small round knob to open it with. I don't know how I knew it was locked, because I never even attempted to open it but, somehow, I just knew.

I was startled momentarily, as I felt someone put their hand on my shoulder. I tried to turn around to see who it was, but I couldn't, and found myself physically fixed to the spot. Out of the corner of my eye I saw a tall, thin, male figure. Not well enough to determine who it was, but I knew it was a man. I realised that I wasn't frightened by what was happening. I felt comfortable as if it was someone I knew. I randomly thought it might be my cousin's boyfriend.

I felt a warmness envelope me, as if I was being held intimately from behind. It felt close, warm, comforting and safe. It was so peaceful that I started to relax into this warm embrace, but

I jumped when I realised I still had no idea who was holding me this way and I started to panic.

A strange man was making me feel loved, and it suddenly felt wrong and that I needed to get out of this situation. I guess abuse makes you wary of love. Before I had time to wriggle free, I noticed his face. He was resting his chin on my right shoulder. The fear in me subsided instantly. He was familiar, but I still couldn't place where I knew him from?

He had long, slightly wavy, dark brown hair. His face was rough and uneven, and his skin was dark. It was very odd to feel such an intimate love from a fairly unattractive guy who I may or may not have known!

It was then that I noticed his outstretched hand in front of me. If you can imagine, he was standing directly behind me, facing the same direction as me with his arm slipped between my waist and my arms so I could see his hands in front of my body.

In his hand lay a large key; the old-fashioned type made from a dull bronze metal, not shiny or special-looking at all. Without him saying a word, I already knew this key was for my cupboard.

As suddenly as he appeared, he was gone, and I was alone in the kitchen staring at the cupboards. I don't know what God had in store for me or what was inside my cupboard. Whatever it was, I knew it was just for me. It was a really strange feeling being loved by someone who obviously knew me, without me knowing them. Maybe I knew him once, but I certainly did not now. However, I couldn't shake how familiar he felt.

Actually, when I think about it now, it seems so obvious, it must have been Jesus. He was behind me because I turned away from Him long ago. But that never stopped Him from loving me or even bringing me something special. There aren't any words to describe how that made me feel. It had been a long time since I felt loved by anyone, let alone by someone I rejected.

I knew I had to make every effort to continue reaching out to him too. He gave me the key to my life, which meant that I could enter something new when the time was right. The key looked so plain and ordinary (a bit like me, I guess), but I knew it held something extremely valuable, and I couldn't wait to see what God would do next.

I never realised how precious the gift inside me was, and how desperately the enemy wanted me to reject God's plans and promises for my life. However, I would soon find out.

CHAPTER 12
My double life

Finding out who I was on the inside was oddly therapeutic and I really was starting to understand the power of God in my life.

However, at the same time, my outside life (where everyone else lives) had become like a war zone. It was like there was a battle for my soul constantly raging and I was caught up in the middle. I was still learning to connect with God, taking time to pray and read my bible, but I was also smoking more crack than I ever thought possible. It's like people went out of their way to give it to me for free and, no matter what I decided, someone was there with money, crack, or both.

This must be what double agents feel like. By day, I was one person; I was mum to a beautiful toddler and a new Christian learning the ropes. At night, once Reece was in bed, my home had a constant stream of visitors from dusk until dawn. It's not like I planned it but, because I had a nice house, it allowed others who 'partook' to use my space in exchange for free drugs.

It is not something I am proud of, but it did have some benefits. I was not spending any money so, financially, I was doing OK. On the downside, I didn't really sleep and, just as the last visitor was exiting my house in the early hours, Reece would be waking up to start the day.

I wondered what God made of all this, as I was desperately trying to consider him in all things, but drugs being thrust under my nose daily was a temptation I was ill-equipped to withstand. Once I hit that first rock, it was like God never existed.

I would start every day by renewing my vow of commitment to God and end each day I promised I would do better the next day. I was feeling confused, as I assumed things were supposed to get better when you became a Christian. However, my experience was, sadly, a stark contradiction to that theory.

I was loving being back at church and in the fold, relearning God's and the Christian way of life. Family connections were getting better all the time and I would spend every Sunday at church with my family, then go back to my parents' house for dinner. Well, actually, I would just go there so I could leave Reece in good hands, while I got some much-needed sleep. I was averaging about five to eight hours per week. Sunday with my parents allowed me to get a mammoth 12-hour sleep, so I didn't lose my mind from sleep deprivation.

The lack of sleep was already starting to cause poor judgement and decision-making. Staying up all night presumably burned calories, because I would spend the rest of the day torn between being ravenous and exhausted. Reece really was a little trooper back then. I had no excuse for what I was doing, other than I was an addict in denial. For some reason, my regular bouts of passing out asleep didn't seem to bother him at all, and he became accustomed to watching TV and playing while I slept at odd hours of the day. I wouldn't discover for many years that I was actually suffering from a neurological sleep disorder, probably triggered by trauma from abuse.

I should be thankful that God blessed me with the perfect baby boy. He deserved the best mum possible, and I knew I was starting to change, but it was taking a little longer than I anticipated. I held tight to the hope that God would help me to work it out so I could focus on being the kind of person my son needed me to be.

Sadly, all my efforts came to nothing, as things went from bad to worse.

My home went from a few night-time callers to a full-on drug dealership in my living room. One of my regular dealers had started becoming pally and had persuaded me to let him use my house for a couple of nights. He paid well, so I was more than happy for the additional free drugs. To be honest, it was kind of exciting, and he was the first man that was not my crazy ex to show me any kindness. However, the kindness came at a very high price. What I didn't know then, is that this was yet another strategy for control. A tactic often used by drug dealers to take control of someone's home called 'cuckooing' - inspired by the only bird that will place its eggs in another birds nest, sometimes pushing the native eggs out of the nest while the unsuspecting bird parent's nurture and raise a cuckoo, rather than their own offspring.

After about two months of this, my night-times became uncontrollable. I had crazy people knocking at my door all night and the dealer started sending his lackeys to sit in my house and manage the business, while he was presumably sleeping. They were loud, rude and disrespectful, which meant I could not relax, and spent the night checking for police and spies. Sleep deprivation and drug abuse was also starting to cause me regular episodes where I would hallucinate, causing me to behave erratically.

In parallel, my stepdad, Richard, was really making an effort to try to guide me by doing a discipleship course with me; teaching me what it meant to really be a follower of God, the fruits of the spirit and how to pray, among other things. I went to church every Sunday, despite not having slept all week and often having been up the night before smoking crack.

I was obviously failing, but I refused to give up trying. I was trapped in this horrible cycle of guilt. Every time I failed to resist temptation, I would use drugs to soothe myself. It was like a form of self-flagellation where I judged myself unworthy and punished myself by doing the worst thing I could. Even when I did well for a couple of days, I used drugs as a treat for being good which, looking back, is crazy but typical of an addict's warped thinking.

This is how the enemy works; he gets us caught up in trying to save ourselves and, when we fail, we judge ourselves, leading us to self-harm. I can't tell you how many people I have seen come to an awful end this way. It breaks my heart knowing that some people never make it, no matter how much you support them. It also makes me value my journey, knowing that I was able to take help when offered, recover and eventually heal.

During all this chaos, I also found a new way to connect with God that came as a surprise. I started singing worship songs at home. I know it doesn't sound like anything amazing, but it created this instant connection with God that helped me to feel less alone in the craziness that surrounded me so often. It was so cute listening to Reece mimic me, and I could feel a tangible peace descend on me, my home and even little Reece.

This whole experience shattered the beliefs I was raised with. I was taught that sin led to death, and as a child, no one really explained what this meant. Serena and I always had a sense of pending dread while growing up, believing that at the slightest wrongdoing, the sky would open up and we would be struck by some sort of holy lightning (I realise now this is more like Zeus than who God actually is).

We learned about God rejecting people who sinned, that God would punish those who sinned against him, and sin of any kind should be repented of before we slept in case Jesus came back in the night and we got left behind at the rapture. Fear, punishment, death and hell were very real threats growing up in our house, and the remnants of those beliefs were being challenged by my predicament. I prayed every day for a way out, so I could be free to follow God the way he wanted me to.

My life was starting to resemble a horror movie, and I seriously began to think I was somehow cursed. I know I keep saying this, and I know it sounds crazy, but I could feel the darkness chasing me. I guess I am one of those spiritually susceptible people who can sometimes feel things they can't see. That, combined with drug abuse and sleep deprivation, was causing serious paranoia.

The drug dealer had taken to leaving his smacked-up gopher at my house. She did the night-time deliveries, while smoking copious amounts of crack and heroin until the early hours, then would crash out in my living room. It was impossible to wake or move her, so Reece and I were sharing the house with a crazy addict, and I had no idea what to do. Once the dealer left for the night, he would not answer my calls. I was torn because they were my free meal ticket. If I made a fuss, I would likely lose my free drugs.

Reece's dad was being a nightmare, as usual, oppressing me with constant harassment, abusive drunk texts and calls. I felt like I was in permanent flight-mode, defending my right to be a living breathing human being. I was at least able to find a little safety at my parents' house. Without them, I am sure I would have done something drastic, but they always provided me with a safe haven when I needed it. Oddly enough, it became one of my coping mechanisms.

My stepdad's response was the biggest surprise of all. After all the bad blood between us (of his doing, I might add), he seemed to have a genuinely caring side, which I never expected. I had already decided I could not let our past dictate our future, so I actively decided to forgive him for what he did to me all those years ago.

I only ever told my mum what he did to me, but after her reaction, I just didn't see the point in telling the truth. No one wanted to hear it, and it had become irrelevant to my current life. What was done was done, and no one could change it. I would never get justice and, frankly, I don't think there was anyone in my life who cared about it. I knew God wanted me to forgive him so I could move forward with my life. Holding on to my past hurt would risk me losing my family for a second time. For the first time in years, we were getting on, and that's all that mattered to me. The invisible strings attached to our relationship had not gone unnoticed, but I decided to live with it.

CHAPTER 13
Under threat

Have you ever had to forgive someone for something so heinous that you don't know if it's even possible? That is the task I found in front of me, and, despite its gargantuan size, I knew the benefits of overcoming it would be worth it. After all, what are we without family?

Throughout all this turmoil, I was semi-estranged from my immediate family, which rendered most of my family relationships strained, except with my sister Serena. There were a number of reasons for this, so I will do my best to explain.

At the age of 15, I rejected my family, their religion and their way of life. This is quite common, as teenagers often seek to exert their new-found independence around this age. For me, it was my only escape.

I can't quite explain the devastating feeling of realising your dream come true is actually a nightmare. At that age, with the restricted upbringing I had, I didn't even know where to begin to understand what was happening, other than it frightened me and I could not live under the permanent threat that lurked in my childhood home.

After being ditched by our birth father, Serena and I were overjoyed to be given a new dad in the shape of our stepdad Richard. He was weird, uncouth and unfamiliar with what to do with children, but that didn't matter to us. As far as we were concerned, our prayers had been answered and we had a new dad. Our faith in a God that does miracles was solidified by the new man of the house.

After a few awkward years, he grew into his dad role and we settled down as another sibling arrived, giving me and Serena a little brother, Taylor. He was super-cute but not a good sleeper, so kept the whole family awake for several years until he learned that night-time was for sleeping. For a time, I was happy and completely unaware of what was lurking in our home.

Looking back, I don't remember night-time being restful at all, although it seemed normal back then. Even after Taylor had learned to sleep, Richard would play pranks on me by hiding his travel alarm clock in my room, forcefully waking me out of my sleep at 2 or 3 a.m., while my bleary-eyed, 10-year-old self would search for the source of this noise. I would eventually give in and wake my parents, which always ended with my mum getting annoyed and Richard hiding his laughter under the bedcovers. It all seemed so innocent back then.

I was already struggling with staying dry at night and had been fitted with an alarmed mesh mat which went under my sheets and would blare loudly if it got wet. The combination of these things led to a pretty unhealthy sleep pattern which would rear its head later in my life.

As the years passed, so did the frequent house moves. It seemed like, just as we got settled, some new job or mission would materialise, and we would be informed that we needed to pack up our stuff and leave. Again.

I remember one particular move (which was the last of three house moves within 18 months) that became the start of the downward spiral. At 12 years old, I was on the verge of teenagerhood and starting to develop in ways that girls do at that age. I had already had 'the talk' with my mum, which I only found out in much later life, was not the same talk everyone else had.

When I was around nine years old, my mum sat me down in the living room to watch a video about sex. Not unusual in and of itself, however, what I assumed was an educational-type video, seemed to shock other people, once I had told them what I watched. The video not only described the act of sex, but showed a man and a woman having intercourse, explaining what went where and how fertilisation happened. I had no idea at the time how inappropriate that was for a nine-year-old.

At age 12, Richard had become extremely familiar and took great pains to publicly discuss my rapidly changing body and what men would soon be wanting from me. Nobody seemed to bat an eyelid and it was seen as a father teasing his daughter. I too thought that this was normal behaviour, as we still lived in a restrictive household, and I simply had no other experiences to draw upon.

As the months rolled by, the inappropriate behaviour and comments continued. I recall being in the car with him and him pointing out a young girl from our church. He said that the stain on the back of her skirt was a sperm stain because she had been having sex. Richard had also begun touching my bottom in passing, even in family settings and paying way too much attention to me. I felt uncomfortable and embarrassed, but no one did or said anything. As far as I could tell, my mum and wider family seemed to be OK with it.

The house we lived in was still being renovated, so until completion, Serena and I shared a room. I loved sharing with Serena; we were like two peas in a pod and everywhere I went, so did she and vice versa. There are only a few times during our childhood that we were ever separate. Once the renovations were completed, I was given my own room for the first time in many years. It was on the ground floor, at the back of the house behind the kitchen and bathroom. This is when Richard started visiting me.

At first it seemed innocent enough. He would pop in and check how I was doing, initiating conversation that seemed genuinely caring. To be honest, it was nice getting some one-to-one attention, which was a rarity in our house. However, things took a turn when he wanted to talk to me about boys and what they were after.

We would be sitting together on my single bed, so close that I could smell his deodorant and aftershave. There was always at least one hand somewhere on my body; my shoulder, my waist, my leg. He wanted to show me what men had between their legs, so I wouldn't be shocked or surprised when it happened in real life. He would force me to look at the bulge in his trousers, while telling me what girls can do with an erect penis and what boys wanted from girls.

At the time, I didn't even know why I felt so uncomfortable. Talking about sex with a parent is probably the dread of every teenager, so why would I be any different? Not that I even had a clue what a typical teenager did. All I knew was what my life was like, and I had no gauge by which to compare or measure my experiences.

Have you ever felt like you were in danger but didn't know why? That's what I felt like growing up in my home. Like being under constant threat, scared of the unknown monster lurking somewhere under the happy facade created by my parents. This went on for a year or so until we moved house, yet again.

We were in a new town, in a new home, new schools, a new church, no friends, no family close by and I felt like I had been dumped into a strange world surrounded by strangers. We lived in a housing project for troubled young people, managed by my mother, who thought it was her godly duty to care for every lost soul, waif and stray she could find. This meant she was busy a lot, occupied a lot, away a lot and generally unavailable. This left me and my two siblings in the care of Richard.

This was not the first time Richard had been the primary carer for me and my siblings. He had sporadically been the 'at home' parent during periods of unemployment and while studying for his pastor's degree. As the eldest sibling, and more than 10 years older than my baby brother, a lot of the caring responsibilities fell on me. I didn't mind, to be honest. It was probably the only thing I was able to do autonomously, so I felt quite gratified by the trust placed in me.

Ironically, I think it was taking those first independent steps into young adulthood that sealed my fate. I was growing up physically and emotionally; a progression that had not gone unnoticed by my stepdad. He started to pay more attention to the way I dressed and would make an effort to check on my progress at school. He would treat me with snacks and (approved) movies if I had been particularly helpful with my siblings. In fact, he went to great lengths to make me feel special and appreciated.

From the outside looking in, and even from my clouded perspective, he seemed like a doting stepdad. This was short-lived, as my life changed when I was awakened one night. Richard came into my room in the middle of the night and said he needed to talk to me. Half asleep, I crept out of the room I shared with Serena, so I didn't wake her, and followed Richard out onto the upstairs landing.

I thought my little brother Taylor had woken up and Richard needed my help getting him off to sleep. But there was no sound or lights coming from his room. We stood in the hallway for a moment in silence, as I waited for him to speak.

He said that he was feeling lonely with Mum being away and couldn't sleep. He said that the only way he could sleep is cuddled up next to someone, so would I mind sleeping in his bed with him while Mum was away. I stood there, frozen on the spot, my mind reeling, and a sharp stab of panic rose up but refused to escape my lips. I don't know if I said anything in reply, or if it would have mattered if I did. He took me by the hand and led me to his and Mum's room across the hall.

He guided me through the dark hallway and across the darkened bedroom until my knee bumped on the edge of the bed. He was standing so close; I could feel his chest hair rub against my arm. He reached around my body to usher me onto the bed and pulled the duvet over me. I remember being petrified and scared of what Mum would think if she saw us. I turned away from Richard as he climbed in bed next to me. My eyes were tight shut as I tried to think. But I couldn't. I couldn't speak, move or think. Richard wrapped himself around me, spooning me from behind, and we stayed like that for a while. I started to feel a small sigh of relief and almost relaxed until he started to push himself in between my legs, until his penis disappeared inside me.

I don't recall much after that, and I don't even remember going back to my bed. All I know is that was the first time Richard had sex with me, and my life would never be the same again.

CHAPTER 14
The viper's den

I have never really shared what happened in detail before. It's as if my body kicked into autopilot and ground to a halt. I didn't know how to process what had happened and I guess shock had me stuck in freeze mode.

I have spent my entire adult life reeling from the events that started on that night. Not only from the event itself, but from how my world responded to the violence upon my black female body. Back then I had never heard of grooming, gaslighting or coercive control but I now know that's exactly what happened to me. The tiny world which had been manufactured and controlled by my parents became a gaslighting zone that followed and preceded me wherever I went for the next 25 years.

The burden of being wronged in this way almost caused me to stay silent. I have had to fight every instinct to share what happened. My drug counsellor seemed to be the only person who saw that broken part of me and tried to do something about it.

I remember after four months of being at Victory House, I had still not broken any rules, so was never punished. I followed the rules religiously. To the untrained eye, it looked like I had got this rehab thing down and that I didn't need much in terms of correction. However, I knew that God opened her eyes to see what was really happening beneath the surface.

Most of the girls who go to Victory House have all kinds of issues with low self-esteem, anger, unforgiveness, lack of self-control, etc. None of those things seemed to fit me, and it became noticeable among my peers, as I strived to be the best at everything; following every order, request and expectation without comment or complaint. I thought I was doing everything right. My counsellor was the only person to spot that, actually, my responses were very wrong.

She was the only one to see that my behaviour was derived from subjugated compliance which is common among those who have lived in long-term abusive situations. It's a kind of survival mode for the severely abused, who adopt a permanent level of compliance to appease their abuser. Of course, this never appeases them, and the abuse continues. However, for those poor souls who experience this level of controlling abuse over a long period of time, it can become difficult to identify the abuse, as the abuser or perpetrator have established an unhealthy codependent relationship that neither party knows how to separate from.

After suffering years of regular night-time visits from Richard, at the age of 15, I finally plucked up enough courage to tell my mum what was happening to me. I remember the event so vividly and it framed my fragile thinking for decades to come.

Richard was out for the evening so I could finally talk to Mum alone. She stood in the kitchen preparing some food for the following day, so there was at least a little distraction from the devastating news I was about to deliver. I explained as best as I could, in my limited way. I noticed that she barely looked up at me, other than to ask if I was sure that's what had happened? I replied that I was sure, and she just said, 'OK,' and continued prepping food for the next day.

There was no visible sign of shock, no tears, no anger, just a cold indifference to my bombshell news. I don't know what I was hoping for, and I assumed she just needed time to think and speak to Richard before responding to me. It wasn't until two days later that my world would come tumbling down.

I had avoided (when possible) any contact or conversation with Richard over the next couple of days. In my mind, Mum would get the truth out of him, throw him out and save the day. I guess that is more a reflection of my childlike mind attempting to find the 'happy ending' in this scenario.

I knew my Mum to be a good and dedicated Christian, so there was no way Richard could get away with it. We had been taught that God always punished the sinful and blessed the righteous. All I needed to do was wait for the punishment to begin. I was completely unprepared for what came next.

After my siblings had gone to bed, I was summoned into the living room, where Mum and Richard, both stern-faced, asked me to sit down so we could talk. My anxiety levels were through the roof and my stomach was churning, not knowing what was going to happen next, but feeling hopeful the nightmare would finally come to an end.

Mum was the only one who did any talking. She asked me why I had lied about Richard in that way, and if I understood the damage I had done to him. Stunned does not even come close to how I felt. I think I must have shaken my head or something, because she didn't even wait for an answer before laying into me about telling lies and the danger I had put Richard in by making a false report of this nature.

I remember looking across at Richard and, I swear, he had a slight smirk as he sat quietly backing my mother, who had burst into tears, apparently ashamed that her eldest daughter could be capable of something so awful.

I don't remember much else about that night except the burning sensation in my eyes, throat and brain as I struggled to come to terms with what had just happened. Serena did her best to comfort me, but the reality is she was scared. Scared of daring to openly stand by the newly christened monster of the house.

All those years of preaching fire and brimstone for the sinners of the world and being told that we were better than everyone around us, because we were chosen by God, all came crashing down at once. My mother now considered me a threat and refused to speak to me for weeks, while Richard spewed venomous looks at me, spending every waking minute trying to make my life more miserable than it already was.

To add salt to my wounds, my parents went to great lengths to portray Richard as the victim of a vindictive and deceitful daughter. I arrived at church – the only place where I had relationships outside of the home – to find disapproving looks, sermons about truthfulness, and that I had all the social pull of a leper.

I later discovered they had gone to the church leaders to pour out their broken hearts about their wayward daughter, who had become a pawn of evil and was trying to destroy their marriage. I remember hearing someone mention that I had accused Richard of molesting me. I had never heard that word before, and it would be many years before I fully understood the term and what they had done to me that day.

I thought Richard was the most evil person in the world, and my forced silence and public judgement broke what was left of my poor teenage soul. After all those years telling me about Jesus, justice, truth and godliness, it all boiled down to nothing but powerlessness in the face of evil. I was now branded a liar, deceiver, attempted marriage-wrecker and had become an overnight outcast at home and at church.

School didn't really count, as I had no real friends there anyway, and my world became a harsh, cold, judgemental place, without comfort, kindness or support from any direction. I was alone in this, and the more I sank within myself, the more I realised I could no longer stay in this home of hate.

At age 15, I packed up my things and left home. It was the day my mum died, and Veronica was born. Veronica, the woman who gave birth to me but refused to be my mum. She chose her wicked husband, Richard, over the safety of her child, and there was nothing I could do about it.

CHAPTER 15
Stolen child

No one teaches you how to get over a trauma. In fact, most people are not even comfortable talking about traumatic events. That is one thing for which I am truly grateful. God listens without judgement, walks with me in those silent spaces, where words are a hindrance and tears blanket the wounds of a broken heart. He did that for me, and I am grateful to God every day, for being the friend and comforter I always needed.

I rarely talk about Richard and Veronica now. They seem like a distant past. The first trauma of many. The first crack of the whip that splits open the skin on your back. The first broken bone caused by a great fall off the mountain. The first lick of flames on skin, in the great crucible of flame.

I thought I could just forget. Pretend it never happened. Fake it. But they wouldn't let me. Years later, Richard wrote several books as part of his pastoring ministry and could not wait to fill it full of lies about my attempt to smear him, how he and Veronica had survived and what a troubled teen I was. Of course, in his version of events, he was both the victim and the saviour.

It made me sick.

Everyone at church and our extended family had a copy of his book. So even those who had put aside what happened were then reminded of what Richard claimed I had done. I was publicly shamed as the black sheep all over again. There was simply no escape for me, other than to abandon and avoid my family for the second time.

Understanding this made my relationship with Grant make more sense. He was a lot older than me (by thirteen years), and he filled an important role of a nurturing adult that I no longer had in my life. Don't get me wrong, I am not unaware of the fact Grant was not always a positive influence in my life and was the person who introduced me to heroin, long before I even knew what it was.

My absolute ignorance of the real world left me like a lamb to the slaughter, allowing people like Grant and Daemon to take hold of my delicate little life in a way that I would never allow now. It's so sad that my earliest memories in this world are marred by evil masquerading as love. It's also sad that I learned this far too late to prevent some of the worst travesties of my life.

One of the saddest things about this whole situation is that I had worked so hard to forgive Veronica and Richard. I had actively and willingly put aside my feelings of anger, injustice and hate so that I could fully give myself to God. It wasn't easy and it was most certainly a process. However, I was committed to building my new life and salvaging what I could of my parental relationships.

I had tried to be fair with Daemon, despite his psychotic behaviour, because I believed it was the right thing to do. Reece deserved to have contact with his father, and more than anything, I wanted him to have a better father experience than I did. It seemed that no amount of being good, or doing good, was able to halt the attacks on my life. It seemed like God was OK with all this shit, and I was beginning to regret my decision to follow God.

I don't share this to point fingers and blame (even though that would be entirely just). I am doing this for myself, to help free myself from the pain I still endure from this traumatic incident. This is something I could never have envisaged in my wildest nightmares. And it reminds me that my entire life, I have had an invisible target on my back that I could not escape. It is situations like this which remind me of my vision in Florida. That I will face insurmountable opposition and obstacles. The only problem this time is holding on to my faith long enough for God to save me.

The Christmas after my Florida trip, like everyone, I was getting ready to spend the holidays with family but especially with Reece who was now two years old. It was Christmas eve and should have been a time of celebration and excitement. Instead, I had left my house after reporting my two-year-old son missing to the police. He had gone to Daemon's for two weeks, but his dad never returned him, would not answer his phone, his house was empty and none of his family would speak to me or give me any information about where my boy was. My family and I spent days knocking, calling and searching for any sign of them, but always turned up empty.

I still don't have the words to describe the pain and anguish of a missing child, especially when you know the person who has them, might as well be the devil himself. I was filled with dread, doubt, fear, anger, and my mind was spinning, not quite able to believe what was happening.

The police were worse than useless. They refused to consider it a kidnapping. Apparently, a natural parent can't kidnap their own child! The most I could do was report him missing and hope they eventually turned up. I had to do that awful thing you see parents of missing kids on TV do and give the police the most recent picture of their child. It took all my strength not to burst into tears there and then. What if the worst thing I could imagine had actually happened?

I desperately tried to trust God, but it seemed like a very cruel and twisted joke was being played on me. God called me and I responded with a "yes." And for my commitment, I am rewarded by someone stealing my child and a police force who don't give a crap about single mums who look like me. The catalogue of destructive events in my life was growing at a pace, not even I could keep up with.

Things hadn't been going well for a while. There was a fire in my kitchen, which rendered it unusable and, despite my love and dedication to God, I just could not seem to keep off the drugs entirely. My ex was an ongoing nightmare, making multiple false allegations about me to anyone who would listen. My life was miserable, and I didn't know how much longer I could hold on to God, if life was going to turn out like this.

Ever since I gave myself to God, evil had clearly been conspiring to destroy me by any means possible. I wanted to fight back, but how could I do anything when I didn't even know where my own son was and there was no one with any power who could help me?

I decided to spend Christmas at my parents' house. I couldn't bear to be at home alone, looking at his toys and clothes and driving myself insane wondering what had happened to Reece.

It was not really much better there, as they were as worried as I was. We all knew my ex-husband was a vindictive bastard, but to do something like this was a whole other level of wickedness.

I honestly never thought he would stoop so low as to separate a child from his mother. I couldn't even think about him. I just needed to find a way I could get through it that didn't involve obliterating myself on drugs and drink.

New Year was maybe the saddest day of my entire life. We had taken down the Christmas tree and I had to pack all my son's Christmas presents into a black bin bag. He was still missing. No one had seen him or his dad except the police. The police had withdrawn from the case, but not before committing crimes at Daemon's behest.

You see, after the fire in my kitchen, I was waiting for the council to make repairs, so it was usable again. It was mostly smoke damage, so it looked worse than it actually was. I found out several days after reporting Reece missing that the two officers who visited the house to take my missing person report had lied on the police records. Yes, you heard correctly, they lied!

The report outlining the situation went something like this:

'Mum has said she willingly gave her child into the care of the father and agreed he should have been returned at an agreed date. After enquiring why, she sent the child in question to stay temporarily with the father, mum claims there was a house fire and was unable to care for the child because of damage to the property. Upon inspection there was no visible damage to the property, and this seems to be an ongoing dispute over child custody.'

This is what it is like being black and dealing with the police. I can categorically tell you that my kitchen was indeed fire damaged. There is no way the police could include details of what they deemed 'no visible fire damage,' as they never left my living room. The assumption was that being black, and a single mum, somehow meant I had either visited this insanity upon myself, was a liar, or was such a poor parent that I had simply given my child away.

I shouldn't have been surprised at all, as this was not the first time police racial bias had reared its ugly head in my life. Only six months previously, I had to call the police after my home was broken into and destroyed, with me still inside. An annoyed neighbour was not impressed by the obvious drug dealing and night-time disturbances coming from my house and had called around, kicking up a stink. Everyone made a sharp exit, leaving me alone at home.

Once they had all left, I heard a loud thump at my front door, and being still high as a kite and paranoid, I ran upstairs and hid in my bedroom. I heard the front door give way, followed by a lot of smashing and crashing, as a very angry man proceeded to use a hammer and smash all my windows, furniture and anything else that he could destroy.

I peeked through the gap at the top of the stairs and spotted my neighbour's boyfriend in destruct mode, shouting that anyone left better get out or he would kill them next time he saw them. I was petrified he was going to kill me with a hammer and, as quietly as I could, I called the police and asked them to send help.

After what seemed like an eternity, two male officers arrived at my house and announced themselves. I gingerly crept out of my hiding spot, clearly shaken, and watched as the two officers crunched their heavy boots through the thousands of shards of glass, now scattered across my house. An old-fashioned house design meant all my internal doors had glass panels, which were now all shattered, along with my front window and various belongings.

After attempting to explain what had happened, one of the officers asked me something I will never forget, as long as I live.

"Are you sure you didn't do this yourself, love? It doesn't look like forced entry and we can see you've been taking something, so perhaps you did it yourself without realising?"

It's not every day you call the police as a victim of a crime only to be accused of committing the crime yourself. Welcome to reporting while black. As soon as I heard that, I knew the rest was pointless. They conceded in giving me a crime reference number and said all I could do was call the council to come and repair the windows.

I told them that I didn't know who had done it, because I was too scared that my neighbour would retaliate and kill me next time. Let's be honest; it's not like the police would save me. I would just be another dead, black junkie who no one cared about. I packed a bag for me and Reece (who was thankfully away that weekend with his dad) and headed for my parents' house, where I knew I would be safe. At least for a while.

We were all traumatised by Reece's abduction. Christmas was a sad, stressful and sickening affair as we tried to eat, drink and be fake merry. All Reece's Christmas presents sat unopened underneath the flickering fairy lights on the Christmas tree. A constant reminder of the horror we were trapped in.

Everything had lost its flavour. Every one of my senses was dull and no matter what I did, my stomach felt like I had swallowed boulders that were weighing me down from the inside. We tried distracting ourselves with christmassy things like food, movies and sugary snacks, but no one was feeling anything like Christmas cheer that year.

My family was already devastated by the constant attacks by Daemon against me, my son and our lives. False allegations to police, social services and anyone who would listen were a regular thing. Each time, allegations proven to be without foundation, but it still forced me to defend myself against the authorities, who investigated me without impunity, happily turning my physical and emotional life upside down, then leaving without consequence, as they discovered nothing but a well-cared-for child.

On Boxing Day, after calling the police call centre again to get an update on my child's missing status, I was eventually told a sergeant would be visiting later that day to provide information about a development. The lack of information made me very nervous. I knew something had happened or they would not be sending an officer out, but they refused to disclose any further details over the phone.

We waited and waited and waited. Eventually, a loud knock on my parents' front door at thirty minutes past midnight brought our collective tension to a head. My mum answered the door and was faced with a 6 feet 9 inches officer in a flak jacket, police radio and all the various gadgets police have on their utility belt. He asked to speak to me, and Mum ushered him into the living room where my parents and I were sitting.

This is where it got weird. He refused to enter the living room and asked me to go to the hallway to speak with him alone. Before I could respond, Mum was straight in there and said that whatever he needed to say, we all needed to hear it (side note: Mum is only 4 feet 11 inches, yet was not even slightly scared of this giant police sergeant, wearing body armour, towering over her in her hallway). He again attempted to convince everyone that he was only permitted to speak to me, and I needed to come out to the hallway, but my parents point-blank refused.

I guess my mum knew this story too. She was a black woman and would have had her own (probably far worse) racist encounters and understood completely the abuse of power the officer was attempting to impose upon me. This would be one of the few times in my life where my parents actually had my back. She told this towering copper that if he wasn't prepared to speak to us all, then he would have to leave, and she would be reporting him. Eventually the sergeant complied, stood in the doorway of their living room and began his report.

They had found Reece who was safe and well with his father. He was not at liberty to say where they were as the father had specifically said not to disclose their location. He was aware of ongoing custody issues and Daemon had already raised concerns about Reece's care with police and social services. The police, Daemon, and social services, had already conducted a child protection meeting and decided at this time, Reece was safest with his father, so he would not be returning Reece to my care. He also claimed that I had called him out of the blue, saying I could no longer look after Reece and that he should live with his father and that I dumped him at the house, without any spare clothing, clearly dirty and hungry. Daemon also claimed that I had decided to make a false report of kidnapping because I had changed my mind and wanted Reece back, which he refused to do because of the condition he arrived in.

With that, the officer said the police would be taking no more action as this was a civil matter, which needed to be dealt with by the court and not the police.

I don't recall much of what happened next, but I do know my parents were up on their feet all yelling at this giant copper in their house. To his credit, he maintained his composure as his name and badge number were obtained amid demands as to where we could challenge this ludicrous decision. The guy had expert-level skills to go and lie to our faces in such a heinous way and, after making it clear he had no intention of pursuing this further, he turned and walked out of the house.

We were all in disbelief and sat crying and fuming at the evil visited upon us by one man. Yes, all this because of one man. One man who refused to let me go. One man who was so egregiously offended at my rejection of him, that he sought to destroy me in any way he could.

I remember staying awake until the early hours in my room at Victory House, praying about Daemon and trying to forgive him for what he did to me. God spoke to me so clearly and let me into a secret I had not known before. I always assumed that Daemon was the result of my own sin and that I was being punished as I deserved. I guess lots of people believe in a punitive God, who punishes and tortures those who go against him. That night in my room, God showed me a different perspective.

I opened my bible to Exodus and began to read about the slavery of Israel, under the oppression of the Egyptian Pharaoh. It was not a new story to me but, that night, something stood out which I had never noticed before. Pharaoh was clearly a stubborn man, always used to getting his own way. I could relate. Daemon was certainly that kind of person. No matter what was visited upon his kingdom, he refused to relinquish his power over God's children. Again, Daemon was treating me in that very same way.

Then a verse jumped out at me:

"But the Lord hardened Pharaoh's heart, and he did not listen to them, just as the Lord had predicted to Moses." Exodus chapter 9, verse 12 – New English Translation.

There is nothing that can prepare you for the feelings of loss, guilt, fear and anger of having your child taken from you. I know it is not a unique circumstance, and many parents who experience this type of separation from their child during a custody battle know the emotional torture all too well. However, the pure injustice that occurred during this time is nothing short of scandalous.

It's bad enough being at the shitty end of your ex's vindictive stick, which saw me warding off multiple false allegations. What I didn't expect was for the authorities to support him.

You often see in movies where the police work with parents to get their kidnapped children back, and it gives you a false faith about what that might look like in reality. In my case, the reality was that the police, who should have been there to protect my son and de-escalate any issues using correct procedure, did not. Instead, they chose to lie, provide false information and pervert the process which could have brought a young child back to his mother.

This reality forced me to acknowledge that the systems of this country were never designed for me to win. If a white, middle-aged, wealthy, man can manipulate and probably pay off law enforcement to lie, falsify reports and create a fake narrative to force me to relinquish my parental rights and get away with it unchallenged, then I had to face up to the fact that this would always be a losing battle. Truth doesn't always win over lies and that miscarriages of justice are probably commonplace.

What I experienced is almost unthinkable, but I am here today to tell you not only is it thinkable, but it's true. Being a black single mum in a white man's world is to be in a place of low expectations, a place of subservience, a place of assumed guilt, a place of poverty, a place of powerlessness, and a place without voice. This is the lived reality of many people like me, who have been served injustice as if it was justice, with no one supporting their rights. Bob Marley's lyrics "Get up, stand up, stand up for your rights" are as true today as when the song was released in 1973.

The next few weeks were a blur that I don't remember much of. I spent less and less time at my house because I couldn't stand the quiet. Every part of the house reminded me of Reece. His toys, the stain on the carpet where he decided to colour it with felt pens, his night light and the smell of his baby shampoo were all triggers to a grieving mother. To compound this, my only coping mechanism was still drugs, and I had less reason than ever before to try to stay clean.

My heart felt broken into a million pieces. I couldn't sleep and could barely eat. Every time I tried to return to some sort of normality, tears would well up in my eyes. I would get a sharp pain in the back of my throat from trying to hold back a cry of pain, and my head constantly throbbed with the pressure of trying to hold my shit together.

Most of the time, I felt like I was going to explode with the pressure building up inside me. I felt like one of those mum characters from a TV drama screaming at the world. This was not fair. After all this time of living my own life, away from God, it is only when I turn back to him that my life turns to shit! I kept trying to pray but all I could manage was a groan which swiftly descended into uncontrollable weeping.

When I was able to, I read my bible. I could at least distract myself for a short time and get out of my own head. I felt that everything had been destroyed and I had no idea how to fix it. Weirdly, being at my parents' house and away from my home gave me the space I needed to connect with God. I wasn't eating or sleeping much at all. I was able to hide away in the attic rooms, listening to music, trying to pray and keep hold of what little sanity I had left. It is from this place of brokenness that the anger grew.

I woke up one day and decided I had had enough. Why was God allowing this disaster to occur? Where was he? Why were our prayers not being answered? And why did he have to take my son? If he wasn't going to answer my prayers, I had to find a way to protest his silence. I asked my stepdad to fetch his clippers so he could shave my hair off.

I know it sounds like a weird way to protest to God, but it was extremely cathartic. As chunks of my hair fell to the ground, it was as if my burdens were falling, cares were falling, hurts were falling. It reminded me of the Old Testament practice of wearing sackcloth and rubbing ash onto the body, as an outward expression of inner grief. Only then, could my grief and sadness be replaced with something new.

It was like a fire burning on the inside of me. It was a mixture of anger, defiance and rage. I must have looked a sight as I was very underweight, my eyes were sunken and dark and I looked masculine with my almost bald head. The girly long hair was gone, and I resembled the bald female warriors of the Dora Milajé from the Black Panther movie, who were fierce, unrelenting, proud and willing to die for their cause.

It was in this place that God opened my eyes and gave me a strategy against the enemy intent on destroying me and everything I loved in this world.

CHAPTER 16
The temple wall

I was getting used to the silence. I was a mother grieving, but without the finality of death. For the first time in my life, I thought of those parents who had lost children. I could finally understand their pain and sympathise. The one thing I had learned was that grief cannot be controlled, it had to be journeyed.

My stage in this journey had turned to anger. I was angry at God, not for letting this happen, but for refusing to bring my son back home. We pray in faith. And when I say we, I meant me, my family and my church. We were all praying, but nothing was happening.

I missed the sweet smile of my baby boy and his infectious giggle. I missed the soft sound of his snoring at nap time and the warm, sweaty feeling of his head on my shoulder. I know God had promised me something, but as I considered his promises, I had to examine exactly what that was?

He did not promise me a trouble-free or perfect life. In fact, God offered me the very opposite. He promised that when I needed Him, he would always be there. All I had to do was look up from my problem and up to the light. If what God said was true, and he could not lie, my only option was to seek his light.

After a few months of Reece being gone, I had changed drastically. I stopped crying. Just stopped, as if my emotion chip went faulty. Instead, I quietly seethed. Not with anger, but with fire. I could feel a fire burning inside me that was hard to describe. Unconsciously, a decision had been made to no longer tolerate this situation. I would petition God until he answered, or I died!

Some part of me felt like I was readying for war, although I was not sure who I would fight. All I knew was that I was becoming hard and fiery, like a Spartan sharpening weapons of war before the battle. It was time for me to pray as if my life depended on it. Pray against the power of the enemy. Pray for God to show himself. Pray without ceasing.

It was late and I was hiding in my favourite attic room at my parents' house. I began to pray in tongues out loud and I refused to stop until the Lord heard my cries. The tears began to flow but they were not tears of sorrow. These were tears of fire. They were tears of war. They demanded to be heard and avenged. For the first time in many weeks, I felt the power of God overcome me and my prayer tongues changed.

I was no longer controlling what was said. God's spirit was interceding through me, and I was at the mercy of his power. After what seemed like a long time, everything became quiet. I could feel a strong sense of the spirit and did not speak in case I disturbed his work in me. Instead, I reached for my bible and opened it.

It fell open in Nehemiah. As I read, the words fell into my heart. It was like breathing oxygen after being suffocated. My mind was clear, and I knew what had to be done.

'But now I said to them, "You know very well what trouble we are in. Jerusalem lies in ruins, and its gates have been destroyed by fire. Let us rebuild the wall of Jerusalem and end this disgrace! (Nehemiah 2:17,NLT)

I knew I had to rebuild the walls around my life. The wall would protect me but served not only to keep the enemy out, but also to provide a safe place for me to grow in the things of God. I was not sure how this would help me get my son back, but at least the Lord had answered me (sort of).

It had been nearly seven weeks since I last saw Reece, and I wondered all the time how he was, what he was doing and prayed that he wasn't missing me too much. I missed him all the time, and my heart, mind and body ached, as if I was internally crying out.

I still felt sad a lot of the time, but I no longer felt lost. God had kept me busy preparing and rebuilding my wall. During my many times of prayer and conversation, he gave me clear instructions to follow. I have and will never forget this mystical time in my life, and the lessons I learned will stay with me forever.

I know I looked crazy to onlookers as I spent days and nights locked in my attic room, speaking in tongues, writing on the walls and pacing like a century on guard. But God was working in me, through me, and galvanising my soul for what was to come. Let me tell you about what God did during that time. I pray it blesses you.

The scriptures God led me to came alive in my inner being. I can't describe the feeling adequately, but I know it was powerful, clear, direct and comforting. Not in the cuddle sort of way, but in the way being surrounded by an army charged with your defence gives you peace and comfort because you are defended and not alone. That was what Nehemiah chapter seven had become for me.

God would rebuild my wall, just like he led Nehemiah to do. My first job was to recruit defenders of the wall. The gatekeepers, singers and priests were integral foundations in the rebuilding process, each with their own specially assigned task. God helped me select people to appoint for each post.

My parents, my sister, one of my aunties and a couple from church were the appointed gatekeepers. The holy words in Nehemiah provided specific instruction to them:

I said to them, "Do not leave the gates open during the hottest part of the day. [a] And even while the gatekeepers are on duty, have them shut and bar the doors. Appoint the residents of Jerusalem to act as guards, everyone on a regular watch.

Nehemiah 7:3 (NLT)

They were responsible for protecting my wall from the enemy. They each had specific times of day where they had to pray both offensively and defensively. God had chosen those who were wise and responsible in the things of God and could recognise the enemy, even if trying to enter under a disguise. These spiritual warriors would defend the wall God had built around me.

After the wall was finished and I had to set up the doors in the gates, the gatekeepers, singers and Levites were appointed.

The role of the singers was given to me and my cousin. We had to sing Psalm 17 and Psalm 18 three times a day, every day. This is something that I had never done before, but something I still do even now. I never knew the power of singing scripture, but when you think about it, it makes complete sense. David wrote the book of Psalms. He was a musician and notes often indicate that psalms were sung to specific tunes of the day. This old way of war was reignited in my life, giving me a spiritual tool I continue to use, although now I do not only use it for battle. I use it for strength, encouragement, blessings, praise and thanksgiving.

This was a particularly strange instruction at the time, as there was no music or tune as far as I knew. We had to rely on God's spirit to guide us and, using the words from these two psalms, we sang three times a day as instructed.

Psalm 17 is David's cry to the Lord for justice, and Psalm 18 his prayer of thanksgiving for the Lord delivering him from his enemies. These were both very apt scriptures that the Lord directed me to. They reflected both the pain and the promise and expressed my heart far better than I was ever able to.

The priests' role was assigned to a couple who pastored, but I had never even met. God told me that the people I needed were known to my parents. I spoke to my parents (who were already aware of what was happening) and they knew immediately who to contact. I gave them a detailed request of what God had told me and asked my parents to pass it on.

To my surprise, the couple were not fazed at all by this odd request from a stranger. They faithfully agreed to intercede for my son and I every day, praying for holiness in our lives. It is still amazing to me that God would call people who had never met me, and knew nothing of me, to battle on behalf of me and my son. I have still never met them and can't even remember their names. Thankfully, God knows, and I thank God for their obedience and kindness in my time of need.

My room had started to look like a crazy person lived in there. The walls were covered in paper where I had drawn the outline of my wall. I had drawn the places where the gates were located and added names of those chosen to protect it and corresponding scriptures to various locations.

The scriptures were alive to me and, although I did not know the end result, I could not dispute the word of God living in my heart, mind and soul. The thing that struck me most was how specific God was, not only showing me the wall, but who he had called to protect it and exactly how that should be done. For the first time in my life, I truly felt like a servant of God. This cycle of prayer, intercession and singing would continue for many months.

I still didn't have my son home. The courts had to hire a private investigator to locate him and his father, to summon him to court. The whole thing was crazy.

The difference was, I knew God was at work. He was building something that can never be destroyed by the enemy again. A wall of protection that will allow me to grow in him, becoming the person that God always intended. I praise and serve an almighty and powerful God who was the same in Nehemiah's time, is the same now, and will be the same forever more.

CHAPTER 17
God's will

Losing a child, even for a few short moments in a crowded shopping centre, strikes fear into every parent or guardian. Caring for a child is one of the most responsible and ignored jobs that we have as humans on this planet. It is an expected role for many and there is very little thought about what challenges you may face as a parent.

Most expect sleepless nights, potty training woes and coping with tantrums as a given. People rarely talk about being a parent without a child. Maybe you couldn't carry your child to term, experienced a stillbirth and are suffering guilt and depression as a result. Maybe life circumstances mean you can no longer care for or be there for your child. Or perhaps you are one of those parents who has allowed a broken relationship to come between you and your children, and it's easier to stay away, than to swallow your pride for the sake of your offspring.

For some of us, we are parents without a child because they died, country borders prevent us from being together or someone has unlawfully taken our child and we are desperately fighting to get them back. This was where I found myself, after my ex-husband Daemon, took our son Reece and disappeared without a trace. It was three and a half months before I had my toddler back home and safe in my arms.

The holiday season meant that there were no legal or court professionals at work and I had to wait until after the New Year to find a solicitor and present my case before a judge. Even this was problematic as Daemon had gone into hiding and the courts had to recruit a private investigator to serve him papers to attend court. Thankfully, I had a sympathetic Judge who saw through Daemon's lies as he tried, unsuccessfully, to discredit me. This would be one of the few times the justice system actually worked in my favour. The Judge ordered that Reece be returned to me and my family, and I waited anxiously for the day that our youngest member was back in our loving arms.

It would have been really easy to ignore or blame God during the time my son and I were separated. But I couldn't. God had left such a lasting impression upon my soul that I couldn't do anything but go to my source. Here are some of the things we talked about during that time.

I was reading through the book of Romans in the bible when God began to reveal things to my heart that helped me to process and understand what I was going through from his perspective, instead of my own limited capacity.

"God is using everything for my good."

I had to keep writing it down in my journal and speak it out loud to convince myself of its truth. I didn't know if I believed it yet, but I definitely wanted to and telling myself the truth seemed the only way to convince my soul that this verse could be real.

"God uses all circumstances for my long-range good and those who love God and are claimed by Him can claim this promise."

I summarised Romans 8:28 in my own words to help make it more real to me. I had to challenge my old mindset and push it into a new way of thinking so that I could trust God.

"God won't leave me to deal with problems on my own. When I don't know what to pray for, the Holy Spirit prays with and for me and God answers. I shouldn't be afraid to pray because the Holy Spirit will intercede, in line with God's will and I need to trust that he will always do what is best. I know that with God on my side, nothing and no one can stand against me."

It's amazing looking back I had such tenacity. I was forcing myself to believe in God's word to make it become a reality in my life. As I continued to read my bible, God continued to use scriptures to reveal yet more hidden truths.

I remember reading Romans chapter nine and being captivated by verse 18 "So then God has mercy on whom he chooses to have mercy, and he hardens whom he chooses to harden." (New English Translation)

I recalled the gut-wrenching realisation that mercy would only be given to me if God had already decided that's what he would do. I didn't exactly have a good track record when it came to God doing me favours and for the first time in a while, I felt small. Not a bad thing necessarily. Many churches and church leaders love to tell us how much power we have because we are special, or chosen, or holy, or whatever this year's 'buzz word' is. And although there is definitely some truth in that, it is also true that we are entirely powerless when compared to God.

I think it's one of the first times I questioned not that God could do something, but if he would?

When I read the line about God choosing to harden, I immediately thought of Daemon. God had already spoken to me when I was at Victory House and had likened my tumultuous marriage with the Children of Israel being held captive by Pharaoh the King of Egypt. In fact, it had been even more specific in referring to Reece as the children of Israel being held captive by Daemon / Pharaoh, with me being given the role of Moses who was sent to plead for the freedom of the Israelite Slaves.

If you read the original story in the Book of Exodus, you will come across a very small verse that is often overlooked when people retell this popular bible story. In Exodus 9:12 it clearly states that God was the one who hardened Pharaoh's heart or made him extremely stubborn, and that God had already predicted this would be the case to Moses.

To me, this meant that God had purposely made Daemon hard-headed, stubborn, and power hungry, and the only way I would get my son back would be through a miracle from God. Reece did not belong to Daemon any more than the Israelites belonged to Pharaoh.

The other similarity was that Pharaoh and Moses both grew up as brothers in the palace, which also reflected the close bond Daemon and I once had as spouses. Just like Moses who discovered his true heritage as an Israelite, I discovered that I was never meant to be with someone like Daemon.

Reece was my responsibility just like Moses was given responsibility for the Children of Israel. I knew protecting Reece would be the fight of my life and if the ten plagues were anything to go by, I was in for a rough ride.

What Daemon didn't know was that he wasn't fighting me for custody of our son, he was fighting God. I knew the plagues would come and that it would only serve to heighten Daemon's resolve, but I also knew that in the end, God would win this battle on my behalf.

This was my heartfelt prayer to God after he showed me what was really happening.

"Dear God,

I trust in you, and I give my life to you. Don't let me be disgraced by my enemies. I won't let my faith waiver but if you let me be disgraced by my enemy, it may cause the faith of others to waiver.

I want to be guided by you and I know your word will lead me towards you. You have been faithful to give me wisdom and specific direction through your Holy Bible.

I have known your love and compassion and you have shown me mercy by forgiving my sinful past. I need to continually humble myself so that you can lead me. I know this means asking for help when I need it.

I know you have gone ahead of me to prepare the way and free me from the traps of my enemies. I know you did not give me a child to own. You only gave me responsibility for his welfare. You have made me his watcher and protector and with your authority, I can carry out the task you have assigned to me.

In Jesus' name, Amen."

CHAPTER 18
Deception

Understanding people wasn't a skill I was ever taught as a child and to be honest, I had a mother who was fairly ignorant of people and their motives. The irony was that she worked with people supporting their physical and emotional recovery. I always wondered how she was able to do this but still be blind to what was happening in her own family and right under her nose.

I did eventually learn about people but in ways that I would never choose to repeat. One of the most important lessons I eventually learned was about deceit. Those who perpetrate deceit, their motives and tactics. Sadly, I learned too late to avoid the pain and scars caused by it, which came at a high price. Having been ravaged by deceit, I now count myself as wise to the schemes and impacts that deceit can wreak on the unsuspecting persons' life.

Maybe you've been one of the lucky ones who have journeyed through life while side-stepping the dark underbelly of deceit. Or maybe you have been witness to its destruction, but only as an onlooker and were secretly happy that it happened to someone else and not you. I do wish I could have walked that path with you but for some reason, God had another plan for me.

The funny thing about deceit, is that despite its huge and potentially life-changing impact, when it first arrives, nobody sees it. It looks like it belongs, so no one ever pays attention or asks the question 'what are you doing here?'

Deception looks like your best friend, your family member, your neighbour, your teacher, and your guide. Deception works like a farm, ploughing and tilling until you are ready to be planted.

But the plants that grow are not your own. You have no idea because the seeds that were planted were intended to mimic your own and it's not until they flower that you have any hope of distinguishing the true from the false.

Deceit is insidious and intentional, and will hide in plain sight. It lies and gaslights to protect itself and brainwashes the most intelligent of us because it craves control.

I love nature and spend a lot of time just watching and listening to God's creation. It always teaches me something about my own nature, God's nature or the nature of humans.

I am not a massive bird nerd but I do know that there are some birds who do not behave like the others. Most birds have a season for mating which results in the laying of fertilised eggs. These eggs are then incubated to term and hatch producing offspring. The offspring are cared for by the parent of their species until they are big enough to fly the nest and the cycle repeats itself over and over.

Did you know that some birds are Brood Parasites? A brood parasite is an organism that relies on others to raise their young and the practice can be seen across several species. A brood parasite manipulates a host of the same or another species to raise its young as if it were their own. There are a number of different strategies that make this possible, but the tactic of the cuckoo is perhaps the most well-known.

Cuckoos are known to lay their eggs in the nests of other birds and do so by choosing a host whose eggs are a similar size and shape to their own. In human terms this is the same as specifically targeting a person because they look a certain way. This has been seen in many serial killers who choose their victims because they resemble someone important to them.

This is the same way deceiver's work. They look for someone who is unlikely to notice, be suspicious or wary of the thing they are trying to sneak under your nose. The cuckoo, however, goes a step further in the deceit and removes the hosts own eggs from the nest leaving only the cuckoo egg in their place.

Imagine if a new parent had their young baby taken and replaced with another without their knowledge. If the babies had similar features and size, would they even notice? We are very good at trying to make things fit our own narrative and it is plain to see that you could chalk up your concerns to sleep deprivation, neuroticism, or a trick of the mind. Once you had cared for and nurtured the baby for a time, you would still love and protect it as if it were your own.

This is what true deceit does. It makes you care about it, protect it and adopt it as your own without you ever knowing that the thing you consider yours is actually an imposter.

This is what I discovered when it was too late. Let me tell you about my cuckoo.

CHAPTER 19
Is this love?

Have you ever been so wrong about something that you were previously convinced of? That is a feeling I have had far too often and despite having a very open and communicative relationship with God, I didn't always hear or understand things in the way they were intended.

My stepfather, Richard, occupies one of those places in my world. My beliefs about a person were drastically changed. I chose to trust him, only to discover that I actually had no idea what was really happening and the truth was more than I could handle.

After experiencing sexual abuse at Richard's hands for so many years and then working so hard to forgive him, I genuinely felt that God was healing my familial relationships. Richard's attentive attitude and spiritual guidance had become something of real value. It isn't surprising that I began to rely on this newly supportive relationship after escaping the ongoing domestic violence from Daemon.

I remember writing a poem for him on Father's Day, in an attempt to express how much his love meant to me. I called it 'Real Love'.

This was my first encounter with 'Real Love'.

After a crazy drug-fuelled night, I remember waking up in an alley. It was dark, cold and wet. I was wrecked and to this day, I have no memory of how I got there!

It was snowing heavily and my limbs felt almost frozen solid. I was scared and thought I would die from the cold. I couldn't really feel my body and I could hardly move.

I managed to drag myself to a nearby house and they called my stepdad for me. He soon came to collect me. By now, I knew that I could trust him not to berate me for my lifestyle. It meant a lot, that even whilst I was going through this very dark stage in my life, he was still there.

Again, there were no disapproving looks, harsh words or name calling. I would have deserved any of these.

Instead, I received a look of compassion and a heart of love. Again, he took me home, wrapped me up, put my feet in warm water and fed me. It took me three days to recover and I am not even sure I ever said thank you to him for what he did.

He never demanded that I repay his kindness. He never judged me but showed unconditional love in a time of crisis.

This particular time in my life was very dark and destructive. I couldn't see an end to the hurt and pain I was experiencing. I could not see the light at the end of the tunnel. All I felt was guilt, shame and pain for my actions and I no longer cared about myself, at least not in the way that other people did.

My stepdad's response was to love, love and love me some more. He showed me kindness when all I knew was cruelty and harm. He kept me safe and he cared enough to come out and look for me when I had been away from home for too long.

He was always overjoyed to see me no matter what stinking state I was in. He allowed me to be myself. I did not have to pretend I was something I wasn't. I was Donna, a drug addict, a victim of domestic abuse, hurting and emotionally dead. He didn't care about any of those things. He loved me regardless and did everything he could to show me.

I often think about those times and imagine that I was swept into a river. The current was too strong for me and I was eventually dragged beneath the cold dark water and began to sink.

I was drowning and my body and my mind had no more strength to fight it. Life had ruined me, or perhaps I had ruined myself? Either way, there was simply no possibility of saving myself.

I sank deeper and deeper, till I could no longer breathe and I felt my chest was going to explode with the battle to inhale and exhale at the same time.

The surface light began to fade and my body drifted downwards. I closed my eyes and I knew the end was near. I welcomed it. It was easier to leave than to face the constant turmoil of 'trying to stay alive'.

Something brushed my face and startled me; I quickly opened my eyes. I couldn't see what it was but it grabbed at me and eventually found something to hold and I felt it pull.

I was barely conscious by now and all I knew was I was moving. I looked upwards but I couldn't be sure. The light began to grow stronger but I could feel myself slipping away.

With the life almost drained from me I made one last attempt to see what would be my final moment. I strained my eyes apart and could see a hand around the top of my arm.

For some reason my gaze never faltered and I could see the shape of an arm. The light was blinding now and the cold shock of fresh air hit my face and my freezing body. I was momentarily frozen. After a pause, I gulped in a massive lung full of air.

I was dragged up the bank and lay there coughing and wheezing to catch my breath. For a few moments I couldn't see and was dizzy from the lack of oxygen. Then through bleary eyes I saw a man. I recognised him. It was my stepdad!

It was at that moment that I understood 'Real Love'.

Not the pretty kind of love where everyone is nice, looks good, smells good and buys flowers and chocolate.

But the kind of love that loves people. Not what a person can do for them. Not how the person makes them feel. But actually love the person!

My stepdad reflected the heart of God in a real way. Not in pious words or platitudes. Not in a meeting or church group. Not by donating money to a cause.

God used him to show me what 'Real Love' was. The kind that loves; even when a person is harming themselves.

A real love that continues; even when you feel hurt by the person's actions. For a brief time, Richard's love for me mimicked God's love for me. He saved my life by giving me love.

How did I lose feeling this intense love for my stepdad? In fact, saying that I 'lost' his love is a little misleading. What actually happened was that my eyes were opened and God allowed me to see the truth of his actions.

To this day, it is still one of the most painful experiences of my life.

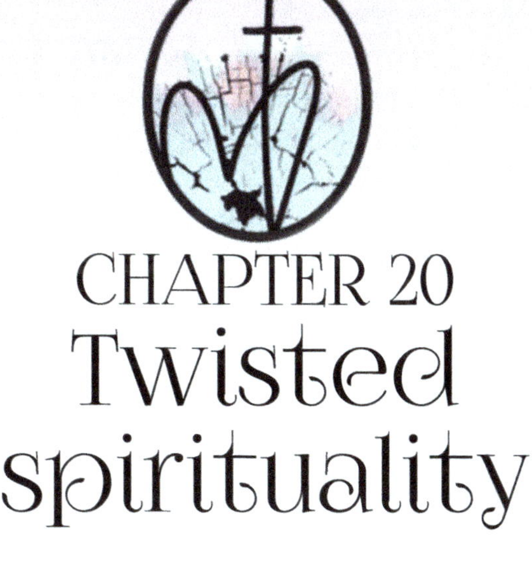

CHAPTER 20
Twisted spirituality

Do you remember me telling you that deceit carefully selects its hosts? I don't know the full story but I do know that I was chosen. What I don't know is if I was the primary or secondary target.

My mum met Richard at a community event through Richard's mum. On the face of it, they had nothing in common. They were different races, from different cultures, had different religions, and had a large age gap with Richard being ten years younger than my mum.

On top of that, my mum was divorced in her thirties, with two children and was a working professional. Whereas Richard was in his early twenties, single with no children, and jobless. They should never have met, yet somehow, Richard made a beeline for my mum and managed to take advantage of a partially opened door.

On the face of it, it looks like my mum (Val) was his intended target but as the insidiousness unfolds the boundary of 'victim' becomes increasingly blurred.

After everything I went through as a child and a teenager with Richard, running away from home at the age of 15 and being separated from my family for many years, I was desperate to find a safe place to heal. For most people that is home and for me it was no different. Despite everything that had gone on, I had the same longing and desires that everyone does. I wanted to belong.

I know that Richard knew this, which is why my parents had already laid down the family unspoken rule which was 'You do what we say or you don't belong'. Not belonging meant being cut off emotionally, not being included in family activities, being ignored to the point where you could be in the same house but neither parent would speak to you. In short, I was excommunicated from my own family.

My excommunication was long-standing and although the birth of my son Reece had gone some ways to allowing me back into the family, I was still very much at arm's length. They would help me practically with bits of shopping or money if I needed it but I had zero emotional support or anything that could be considered loving.

After everything that happened with the abuse at home, being on drugs, being abused by my husband, and my son being taken, I was shattered to my very core. My strength had left me and I guess I was traumatised. This left me extremely vulnerable and Richard wasted no time in taking advantage of a broken and hurting young woman for his own gain.

I had recently recommitted myself to God (only a few months before Reece was kidnapped) and had started attending my parents' church. When I say their church, I mean it was a church held in a local school room, led by Richard who had now become a qualified pastor after completing an online theology course.; fondly referred to as Pastor Rick by his congregation. In attendance were my parents, siblings and several family friends who had known my family for many years, and some other people who I would come to know in time.

It seemed fine and my baby and I were welcomed into the flock and for a while I actually felt safe and supported. My faith began to grow, I was reconnecting with my family and it felt like life was settling down and I could actually start to rebuild my life.

Now I was spending more time with the family and at church, Pastor Rick decided it was time for me to be mentored spiritually; a common process for new or returning Christians so that they can be guided in the basics of the Christian faith. It had been a long time without my family and to forgive Richard for his past transgressions. I knew this was expected of me, so I worked hard to make sure my actions reflected that.

I had been facing the world alone and I was battered by life, so having someone who could show me God's way and a better way was somewhat appealing. I reluctantly agreed and was soon in a small group with three other new Christians learning about fundamental Christian principles and how to apply them to my life.

It wasn't long before Pastor Rick began to take a special interest in me...again. I was obviously cautious but walking by faith and living in my new-found forgiveness, I felt I had no choice but to treat him with respect and the little bit of love I could muster. I simply didn't have the energy to hate and I loved being back in the fold and didn't want to risk losing my place in the family again by doing anything that could be perceived as rejection, bitterness, or unforgiveness.

Richard knew this and took full advantage.

Our meetings started with a small group and we studied the bible, prayed and discussed various topics. All the usual things you would expect from a small church group of new Christians. After a while, Richard decided that I needed more for my spiritual growth and I felt like I had no choice but to say yes.

He started with pre-arranged visits at first and taught me all about the Holy Spirit and God's ability to speak to us through him. To be honest, I loved it at first and committed to connecting with God through the Holy Spirit. My faith was genuinely charged as I began to seek God for myself.

If you didn't already know, Richard was into the long game. Something I now know but was unaware of then. He would groom for years in order to manipulate and brainwash people to bend them to his will. I realised this many years later after suffering from a range of sleep disorders and the sound of an alarm clock gave me a PTSD flashback.

I remember when Richard and my mum first got married, the home was pretty fun and playful and as a family we would often play practical jokes on each other. One of Richard's "jokes" was to hide an alarm clock in my bedroom and set it for 2 or 3 a.m. so I would wake up confused, disoriented and unable to find where the noise was coming from.

Eventually having to wake my mother and Richard to help me find it. Richard would be sniggering under his quilt while my mum would be grumbling about the nonsense and being woken up.

It sounds hilarious and harmless, however, when you know the full story, it stops being funny. He played this joke on me regularly from the age of nine right up until he woke me in the night to sexually abuse me at the age of twelve.

Now the joke is that no one knew he was training me to wake up in the middle of the night, so that he could get access to me when everyone else was asleep. He played the long game and set me up for a lifetime of sleep disorders, sleep deprivation and poor health caused by lack of sleep. Anyway... I digress.

I was genuinely enjoying re-learning my bible fundamentals and doing this with Pastor Rick really helped to cement my forgiveness towards him. I wanted my family back and I had them. Rick was being genuinely attentive and caring and I was feeling the benefits of some one-on-one time with someone who knew more than I did. For a while, I felt like I was actually safe again. Safe from my past, safe from my ex-husband, and with people who genuinely loved and cared about me. I was getting more time with my siblings and reconnecting with them was amazing as I had missed them so much.

This carried on probably over six or seven months before I got my first weird request from Richard. He rang me out of the blue and told me that God had told him I had a message for him and to call me. I was dumbfounded as I hadn't heard from God as far as I knew but the pressure I felt, even from the other end of the phone, was immense. Rick had no doubt in his mind that God had given me a message and stayed dead silent on the other end waiting for me to deliver it.

I can't explain how it made me feel to be on the end of the phone, with such a great expectation hanging over my head. Part of me wanted to believe I could actually hear from God but, another part of me felt like I was drowning from the immense weight of such an expectation and I froze; unable to speak or think. Rick just kept waiting. After what felt like an eternity he simply said, God has given you a message. You need to listen. Go away and I will call you again later.

I knew he would call me and that this wasn't going away. The funny thing was that Rick didn't know who I was or what God had intended for me. That one incident drove me into my spiritual place where I would eventually learn to hear God for myself.

It didn't happen for a while and as with all children, we don't always listen well, so it took some time for me to trust what I heard from God. I can honestly say that I thank Pastor Rick for this as it was the first building block to my real spiritual relationship with God, despite its shady intention.

This continued over the next few months but became even weirder when he asked me to beat him up one night. Yes, that's right, physically beat him!

He was well aware of the history of violence and domestic abuse in my marriage. I was still married, as my ex refused to divorce me. Yet another tactic that denied me my freedom and gave him continued control over me. Richard claimed that God had laid it on his heart to teach me how strong I was.

OK. It sounded like a good thing I guess, and having nothing to really compare this strange request to, I made arrangements to go to the family home and discuss it. I never really thought about it before, but my parents' home was a huge Victorian house on four floors and it was rarely empty. But when I arrived to speak to Richard, the house was empty.

Looking back, it was yet another sign of his insidious way of isolating and manipulating me by making sure there was no one around to challenge him or help me.

He took me into the living room and told me to punch him. I thought he was joking but then he just stood there staring at me (he did that a lot) saying nothing. I felt the air get thick and it was hard to breathe, so I started to panic. I was alone. There was nowhere to hide and no one to help me.

I refused multiple times but he told me that I wouldn't be able to break free from the devil's grip on my mind and spirit until I obeyed him and did what God had asked. He told me that this would set me free from Satan's stronghold on me.

I guess that could be true? After all, I had spent months with Pastor Rick now and I was starting to see the benefits for living God's way. I was back with my family and Rick had gone out of his way to spend time with me, train me in the faith and done so at a time when I had very little love in my life. (Another tactic of predatory abusers).

I was still being abused by my ex-husband in various ways and my time with Richard had become something I really looked forward to. It was something that was building me up, encouraging me and deepening my faith. So he must be doing this for my good, right?

I refused for over an hour and then decided to go home but he wouldn't let me leave the house until I had done what 'God' had asked of me. He said my refusal was me rejecting God's freedom. That's a heavy price for exercising my right to choose, and I was beginning to feel that drowning sensation again.

After some yelling on my part and Richard attempting to make light of the situation, I caved in. I just wanted to go home and if the only way to do that was to beat the crap out of this jerk, then great!

I half-heartedly punched him in the stomach, and he looked at me wryly as if to say, 'is that it?' He started taunting me which I tried to ignore because I really wanted to escape and go home, but he was standing in the way of that. I punched him again but with much more force that he stumbled back. Now he started encouraging me and telling me where to hit him.

I remember punching him hard in the face making him clasp his jaw then swinging my leg to kick him in the thigh. After that everything is a blur but I can see him on the floor and I am kicking and punching him all over his torso and legs. I don't remember getting home that evening but I do remember how shook up I was and the horror of being forced to physically attack someone, supposedly at God's will.

Every daughter instinctively trusts their father and I was no different. Even terrible fathers who repeatedly break their child's trust, still benefit from their child's desire to love and be loved.

Children will tolerate and defend some of the worst and abusive parents because that's all they have and all they want. Stockholm Syndrome is also a common occurrence in abused people who develop a strange addictive love for their abuser through brainwashing and isolation.

This is how typical abusive relationships work. They prey on the vulnerable, groom them into what looks like a loving relationship, and push the boundaries of that relationship until they can take what they want by force or coercion.

Just like the cuckoo, planting their egg in another bird's nest, it eventually produces an imposter that destroys all the other eggs. ensuring it is the sole recipient of all the resources provided by the nest parent.

Richard was the imposter egg, planted into our family nest. When he 'hatched' he went to work destroying anything that would challenge his 'reign' over the nest ensuring he was crowned sole proprietor and could do whatever he wanted to the offspring while my mother kept him fed and cared for, as if he were her own.

CHAPTER 21
Trapped

Life is full of doubt and disappointment, but if we learn to see ourselves through the eyes of God every day, it can transform those negative, destructive thoughts into something that nourishes and blossoms. If we can learn to distinguish between the mind of God and the mind of Satan, we will be better prepared for the battle of the mind, that is life.

I was completely broken and on the verge of taking my own life when I cried out to God. I wholeheartedly believed he would ignore me because I had once rejected Him. Instead, I experienced the power of God's love and he allowed me to see me, from his point of view. He showed me that I had the spirit of a bear.

I believe that God created us all with an individual and instinctive spirit that moulds our character. This spirit is a natural part of us but, as with anything that is left in human hands, it can be damaged, distorted and even destroyed.

God has always spoken to me in pictures, dreams and visions and this next story is one of those encounters.

This particular one started as a daydream. People are often discouraged from daydreaming but I have found it a perfect place to allow God to impress his thoughts over mine and share his wisdom in a way that isn't quite describable in human words.

In my daydream, I imagined that a female bear had given birth to a cub. She spent the next important months of this cub's life teaching it how to hunt, clean itself and how to live in its environment. This young cub was me, growing up safe in the care of my mother, learning, playing, and living a happy existence in the shadow of this mighty creature.

Upon entering the teenage years of life, the cub becomes more interested in the wider world, often leaving the mother's side to explore the woodlands and walk by the stream, happily playing in the water and chasing smaller animals for fun. This idyllic life seems to hold no danger. In fact, the adolescent bear does not yet fully understand the dangers that lurk beneath the beautiful exterior of its life.

Also living near the woods are travellers. Families who live by trading what they can find and entertaining passers-by for money. One profitable trade is in bear dancing. We all know this to be a cruel trade that is now outlawed, but these people are not followers of popular culture. They follow their own culture, separate from society and under their own set of rules.

Catching bears is dangerous but worth it for the ongoing profit to be made. Bears look domineering but are defensive creatures who don't usually attack unless provoked. The travellers know you cannot catch a bear by brute force, so had to be cunning. This meant certain danger for the young bear.

This simple imagery reflected my life. I knew nothing of the world and its many dangers, and I was unprepared and defenceless against the wild world I was exposed to.

A bear is wild and free. It understands other creatures in the forest are wary of it but does not yet understand why. It knows nothing of its own awesome strength and has never had to use it. The bear's mother has always been there to protect it. Its biggest difficulty is learning to fish for food or climb a tree to find berries or honey.

Honey! We all know this as a favourite food for bears. It is with this love of honey that the travellers prepare their trap for the young bear. They have been tracking it from a distance for some weeks to establish its patterns. They know when its mother is far from it, so they will not be attacked by an adult bear when they catch the adolescent. They fill a large bowl full of honey and hide it just out of sight. They leave trails of honey in every direction, all leading toward the trap.

Their nets and metal traps are set and they lie in wait. The bear wanders by his usual play spot and smells the honey. He begins to follow the scent. All sense of safety leaves the bear as he searches for the delightful honey. The scent gets stronger as he gets closer to the overflowing bowl. At last, the lovely, sticky, sweet honey is his. He enjoys a few mouthfuls, spilling honey over his thick brown fur.

The travellers do not move on him yet. They don't want to startle the bear, as that would put their lives at risk. Instead, they patiently wait for the right moment. They waited for a long time and allowed the bear to eat his fill. They knew once the honey was nearly all gone and the bear would be full and sleepy, letting its guard down, that would be the perfect time to pounce.

They slowly crept closer to the unsuspecting bear, armed with a bear trap and nets. The bear, happy in his ignorance, was relaxed and began to doze next to the bowl. He never heard the quiet whisper of the travelling men who were drawing dangerously close to his position.

There was no noise. Then suddenly, the bear realised something was hindering his vision. He was draped in a large net but was still unaware of the imminent danger. The men had cleverly stayed behind the bear so he had not yet seen them.

The young bear began to wriggle around to try to escape the tangles of the net but only succeeded in making it grip more tightly around him. He began to cry and moan and the struggle became more violent. The bear did not understand what was happening.

A horrendous pain shot through the bear's paw and it let out an almighty roar. The powerful roar shook the surrounding trees, but it was too late.

A metal bear trap was clasped tightly to his paw, there was blood everywhere and the flesh was torn. Every attempt the bear made to try and free himself only resulted in self harm. After an hour of struggling, the bear, distressed and exhausted, collapsed, semi-conscious on the grass.

It was then that the travellers revealed themselves. The young bear was frightened and did not know if the travellers were friend or foe. He growled and snarled every time they got near. However, the travellers did not mock or torment the bear further. They just left him injured and went close enough to inspect the animal but far enough away that the bear was not able to do them any harm.

The bear was injured badly during his capture and now walked with a limp. He had given up trying to escape. The sheer exhaustion and pain left it debilitated. If he pulled on his restraints, they gripped tightly against his throat, almost suffocating him. Food was only given after each performance and, the rest of the time, the bear was alone in a cage with no light.

After suffering months of cruelty, the bear began to think of his days wandering the forest and playing in the glades. Was that life just a dream? Would he ever get back there? What would become of this now mangy and belittled creature? Would he ever know the strength within him?

Despite the dire situation, something inside the bear forced his thoughts to change. All of a sudden, he knew he had to escape this cruel prison at all costs, even if it meant death. Death was better than the indescribable horror he was living.

The bear thought about how he was going to escape. He could not break his restraints without causing more pain and damage to himself, and the bars of his cage were indestructible.

Before each performance the travellers would dress him in a costume ready for the people to laugh at. To do this, they had to take off the ropes and chains that bound him, but they stood armed with weapons in case he attacked. This would be the time. He knew there was a risk he would not survive if the travellers attacked, but it did not matter anymore. Freedom was his only goal, at any cost.

The travellers arrived in time to dress the bear for the show. There were at least five of them armed and prepared to attack the bear at the slightest flinch. He had experienced this many times before. He was taken behind the living area while they tugged at his limbs to position them correctly to fit the costume.

Something reared up inside the bear. It was like a white-hot heat that emanated from every fibre of his being. He let out an almighty roar and bared its sharp teeth in a position of defiance against the travellers. They were taken aback and immediately began to beat, whip and stab at the bear. He refused to back down. The pain was no worse than what the bear already felt. He stood on his hind legs for the first time and towered like a great building and swung his extended claws with the force of his whole body.

He heard a scream and a thud, and then something sharp bit into his back. A knife or other sharp instrument was protruding from his shoulder. He ripped it out and lunged towards the nearest traveller, then bore down with his great fangs into the nearest fleshy part. There was more blood, and the feeling of terror had become like a thick soup in the air. What happened next was a blur, but somehow, the bear was running.

Everything hurt, but it was more of a numb pain. There was shouting and screaming and objects were flying through the air like missiles toward him. He could see the trees and smelled the forest for the first time in a very long time. The smell was like nectar to a honey bee; the lure spurred the bear on and he never looked back once. I don't know how long he was running, but eventually the screaming all but died out, the sky began to darken and he was in the forest, alone.

The wild bear who had been hurt and abused was finally free again. His wounds made his movements slow, and sometimes he couldn't catch food to eat. This made the healing process slower as he trudged aimlessly through the forest, sleeping when needed and eating what he could find. Right now, he would be an easy target.

Despite the odds being stacked against him, the bear wandered through safe pastures allowing him to sleep and rest. He ate berries from a bush and found nuts and roots left behind by other animals. He stumbled upon a pool of refreshing water and the sun warmed his back. Once again, he began to hear familiar noises that took him back to happier times and he was glad to be free. He heals slowly and still limps but he is alive.

CHAPTER 22
The spirit of a bear

The story of that bear cub accurately reflected my life. I had spent many years living in the shelter my parents created for me. I knew nothing of the world and its many dangers, and I was unprepared and defenceless against the wild world I was exposed to.

My life during this period was fun, or so I thought. I had left home and was beginning to experience the world for myself but I had no idea of the dangers that were out there. I was soon caught up in a life of drugs and crime believing I knew what I was doing.

I married the man who played the role of the traveller who captured me. I was enticed by money, status and promises of getting anything I wanted. It was not until much later that I knew those things came at a price and the price was me.

The start of my relationship was full of joy and contentment but was short-lived and replaced by a sharp shock of reality. My marriage proposal was something out of a movie and resembled a dodgy deal rather than a request of marriage born out of love. I felt I had been tricked but I couldn't work out if I had been tricked by him or me?

I think it was a combination of trickery from him and gullibility on my part and the fact that I did not know that people could or would treat each other this way.

I was forced to abandon my family; I was never permitted to leave the side of my new husband, which had us linked by some invisible rope.

Violence had begun to regularly erupt and I lived in constant fear of offending the man that I loved. I was trapped. Just like the bear, I allowed myself to be lured by his winning personality and affluent lifestyle. When people were around, he treated me like a queen.

We ate at restaurants most evenings, went clubbing six days out of seven, had drugs on tap, holidays abroad and regular weekends away. He ran his own company, so in my mind, he was somebody. I was taken to important meetings and paraded around as arm candy, hobnobbing with the semi-famous people in his small world.

On the flip side, I had no personal space. I was told where I was going and with whom, what I should wear, how I should speak and to whom. I wanted to tear my own arm off just to escape, yet to an outsider looking in, I had a great life and nothing to complain about.

I was surrounded by people as long as they were approved by my husband. Any old friends I had before we met were told to get lost, and I was never permitted to speak with them again.

This was monitored by vetting my phone calls and checking every call made from my mobile every month.

Even trips to the bathroom were supervised. I was not only escorted, but he sat in with me, as if he was doing it because he couldn't bear to be without me even for a moment. It was a sick way to live.

After years of living like this in an abusive, overbearing, belittling, degrading relationship, I reached a point of despair. I knew that nothing mattered any more except my escape, at any cost. I was worn down, frightened, angry and my mind and heart were both destroyed. I had only one hope of survival. I had to get out!

For many years, I thought the way I was treated was OK. However, I eventually got to breaking point and deduced, I was not created to live that way. Something inside me just clicked and my beliefs about myself and the way I should live, drastically changed.

Don't get me wrong. I did manage to escape, but the repercussions of that life still haunt me to this day. Some of my experiences will haunt me forever. I have mental and emotional scars and silent battles that no one else knows about as a reminder of my trauma. Healing has been a long and eventful journey which I expect will continue for my lifetime.

I believe God gave me the spirit of a bear. I grew up not knowing who I was or that God had created me to be strong, powerful and graceful. My harsh experiences forced this part of my nature to the surface, ironically contributing to who I am today.

Life tried to crush and destroy me, but instead created the perfect conditions to release my true inner person. I can finally thank God for the terrible times in my life knowing that they birthed something indestructible and amazing in me. I had been forged by fire.

I believe God gave me the strength to endure my trials, which brought out the power in me that was already there. This belief has helped me to understand who I truly am and what I am capable of.

CHAPTER 23
Hunted

After leaving Victory House, I was very blessed to be able to stay with the lady who paid for my trip to Florida (where I had my first waking vision). She was a friend of my mother and she opened her home to Reece and I, so we had some support while I attempted to find my feet in my new world.

Whilst there, I attended her local church and did my best to fit in with my new church crowd. This was no easy task as it was a very large church with predominantly white, middle-class families. This wasn't a bad thing in and of itself, however, there were some challenges with churching alongside sheltered and ignorant people.

My first sign that this wasn't going to be a fun and fulfilling episode was when I was told by leaders that I wasn't allowed to be in a room alone with a man. I was mostly confused by this request but later discovered that the prevailing assumption was that all female addicts were prostitutes. Ergo, I couldn't be trusted around men.

Aside from being ignorant and rude, I already knew that my skin colour would influence everything I did or said at this church, so my expectations were kept extremely low. Thankfully, I wouldn't have gone near most of them and getting jiggy with someone was the furthest thing from my mind. However, being perceived as a threat simply because of my gender, race and perceived character flaws was vexing to say the least.

Thankfully, the one saving grace about this new church was that they ran their own drug rehab for men. This meant there were at least some people who didn't have a picture-perfect upbringing, multiple holidays per year, gap years in some African country or pretend that they had any idea of how most other people lived.

This is where I met the man who would become my second husband. He had recently completed his time in rehab and we were both attending the same church but we both felt excluded because of all the things I already mentioned. We quickly bonded over our shared history of drug addiction and our 'fish out of water' syndrome at the big fancy church.

I would love to say it was some big romance, but honestly, we were friends for a long time before we ever thought about a romantic relationship. Truthfully, Luke was a way out of a bad situation that no one ever knew I was in.

Once I was out of rehab, Richard was very quick to pick up our relationship and continue our spiritual mentoring. My trust in him had grown over the years and by actively following God's instruction to forgive those who sin against us. What I didn't bank on was that Richard would use this against me.

I didn't know it at the time but Richard was cold, calculating and premeditated and I was like a blind lamb to the slaughter. Let me enlighten you.

In between the busyness of my days, relearning how to be a mum, organising my life, setting new priorities and reworking my boundaries, Richard was always there. Whenever I felt annoyed with nonsense from my church leaders or felt lonely because the church insisted on protecting themselves from me, Richard was always there.

The only person who consistently went out of their way to make me feel seen and heard, was Richard. This emotional onslaught was a form of love bombing and dissolved my misgivings. I genuinely felt we had turned a corner in our relationship and was enjoying my new relationship with him.

The stepdad I had always longed for, was materialising before my eyes and for the first time in decades, I started to finally believe that God had good things planned for my future.

Even Daemon had started to calm down. We had settled into a court mandated routine that specified Reece not only visited his father at weekends but that Reece lived with me the rest of the time. This was to prevent a repeat of Daemon refusing to return my son after a visit. I was feeling very grateful for this. after experiencing such a trauma.

During this period, I was also being disturbed by intense and often lucid dreams and nightmares that left me confused, sleep deprived and searching for meaning in things that were probably undiagnosed PTSD.

In one dream, I remember being at a party but not the usual kind with music and dancing. This was a far more sombre affair and I didn't know everyone there. I spotted my ex-husband Daemon, with a drink in hand (as usual), but he was a lot more reserved than usual and didn't pay much attention to me at all. When I looked around, I noticed that something was off. Everyone was quiet, reserved and sad. That's when Daemon told me that this was his wake as he had been diagnosed with stomach cancer but he wanted to have his funeral while he was still alive.

This dream stayed with me for weeks and I remember relentlessly asking God if Daemon would die and if what I had seen was a premonition of sorts. I can't lie, I would have been delighted but I was too occupied with the vivid way in which I was experiencing these episodes.

I know I was afraid often, even though I never really acknowledged it out loud. However, my dreams gave me away. I remember waking up screaming and in a cold sweat after being chased by a pack of wild cats during a nightmare. It's safe to say that me and sleep were not on good terms. To make matters worse, the lady I was living with was constantly being disturbed by my night time screams and groans of terror.

Richard was always there to offer me a listening ear and words of advice. We talked about obedience to God being a key factor in living my new life and that this obedience should be extended to our church leaders who God had placed in authority. He made it seem like a perfect and godly picture.

He would also ply me with 'instructions from God' knowing I truly believed it was for my good and that I was prepared to do almost anything to change my life situation. He used my own desires against me and manipulated me to implant thoughts and ideas into my thinking.

He did this by providing interpretations for my dreams, telling me they were warnings from God to stay away from people and encouraging me to isolate myself.

At the time I thought that God was protecting me and using my stepdad to do it. What was actually happening, is that Richard was forcing me, by coercion, to isolate myself from others. This naturally pushed me to engage more in my relationship with Richard. This is a common tactic used by abusers.

After spending months isolating myself, it was easy for Richard to start planting his evil seeds in me. He focussed a lot on my healing and how broken I was after my abusive marriage and that healing would take time. Of course, he was here to help me every step of the way.

Here's what his 'help' looked like.

Arranging for me to spend time alone with him. This included arranging my live-in landlady to look after my young son, so he could take me out and spend time with him. Because the landlady was a family friend, she had no issues with supporting my rehabilitation in this way.

New friends were always met with cautionary bible tales about how wicked people were and could not be trusted. Yeah, I know the irony! This was then followed up with pressure to 'let them go' because they weren't in God's plan for me.

Trying to be a good and obedient Christian, made it easy for me to believe these things. Coupled with my tragic backstory, it was easy to believe that people were mostly bad. All of course, except for Richard!

I was soon in a situation where these 'meetings' were being arranged without my knowledge or agreement and Richard would turn up, having already made plans to have Reece looked after and I would just be whisked away. I didn't know what to do or who to tell and I began to feel like I did as a teenager all over again.

This came to a head when on one of these occasions, Richard took me out for a meal and then to a hotel. I was totally panicked as he tried to reassure me that this was part of my God planned healing and I needed to trust him.

I was starting to feel like I was drowning again. He kept telling me that for me to heal from my abusive relationship, I needed to be loved by a man who genuinely loved me. Without reading anything too weird into things, it made sense, especially as I was now wearing Richard's wedding ring.

He had given me his old wedding ring, after he put on weight and couldn't wear it any more. A gift to me as a sign of his love and commitment to me. Yes, this was the same ring he married my mother with and was now snugly on my finger as a keepsake from a loving stepdad.

I know what you are thinking. I was thinking the same but I was now stuck in a situation, manufactured to keep me trapped. I had no choice but to try and pretend like I wasn't scared of what was coming next and I put all my trust in God to keep me safe.

Richard told me that for me to receive healing from my abusive relationships, I needed to have sex with him to make me pure and whole again. It would give me a true example of love.

That first night in the hotel, I refused to get on the bed or get undressed. He said that I needed time to become more relaxed with him, so instead, he made me watch him shower. Naked.

This is when I decided I had no choice but to move. Living with my parents' friends was giving Richard full access to me and I could not think of another way to close that door. Telling the truth had blown up my life and I was just starting to live again after that bombshell.

CHAPTER 24
Hide and seek

When I finally moved into my own place, I was excited to start my new life and build towards my future. I had applied to university and would be starting soon while also volunteering with a local charity.

Having the freedom and autonomy to build a new life was something that I was more than ready for. I also thought I would be safe from Richard because he would no longer get access to me via our family friend.

How wrong was I! Instead of blissful freedom, I was alone, in a new home with nothing to stop Richard just turning up, unannounced at my house demanding to continue our 'spiritual guidance' meetings. I couldn't seem to shake him out of my life. Either living with someone who inadvertently supported his actions, or now, living alone with no one to protect or defend me from his vile pursuit.

I kept reading bible verses about God's protection and asking when it would be my turn to be protected. It seemed like everyone else found a way out, except me. I felt like I had no escape.

I had already tried telling the truth and speaking up and that had totally backfired and left me without a home, my family or any support so I definitely wasn't going to do that again.

Everyone who knew me and my parents, raved about how amazing and godly they were. Telling me how blessed and lucky I was to have such amazing support from my family and that God really was looking out for me, despite my sinful past.

This was all happening at the same time that I met Luke. We were both lonely in our new-found church surroundings. Nearly everyone seemed to have money, land, perfect families and large houses. The car park looked like a car dealership on Sundays. They were lovely people, but not our people.

We started hanging out and before long became fast friends, watching movies together, attending church and killing the boredom and loneliness of life with each other. I really had no designs on being more than friends and I don't think he did either. We remained friends for well over a year before we decided that we might want more.

It was a difficult time for us both. Luke was battling long term health issues, caused by his previous addiction and I was silently battling Richard, who continued to be relentless in his pursuit of me. It was suffocating.

For the next few months, Reece, Luke, and I did life together. As we grew closer, Luke began to help me look after Reece when I had to leave early for work or attend university. It was nice to finally have someone who could be there daily, help me not feel so alone and identify with the pains of life.

It wouldn't be until six months later, that Luke and I decided to pursue a relationship. I was ecstatic. I had always wanted to be married and now I had found a man who shared my faith, had already shown commitment to me and my son and I had a genuine affection for him.

Luke was very active in church. He served in the soup kitchen, would preach to locals in the town centre and talked about God and being saved from his past all the time. Regularly proclaiming he had been 'delivered' from drugs, smoking and pornography. He was a proud Christian, and I found it inspirational.

This is one of the things that attracted me to him. He wasn't afraid to share his faith, he was honest and open about his past problems and seemed to be wholly committed to God and church. As a newly divorced woman with a child, I thought he might be my answered prayer to finally bring me a Christian man, who I could follow and would love me and my son. However, I was very careful not to rush into anything and committed to spend the next few months praying and asking God to confirm if this was the man for me.

I was desperate for Luke to be the man. Not just for me and my son but also to escape this nightmare of Richard hunting me down like prey. I don't think I was consciously aware of that at the time but looking back it seemed obvious.

I don't know if you have even experienced being hunted but it leaves you filled with constant fear and anxiety. You are constantly in fight, flight or freeze mode which impairs your ability to make decisions. For me this manifested in slightly obsessive behaviours of searching everywhere for a 'sign' that Luke was the man God wanted me to marry.

I would stay up late in the night, reading scriptures, searching for any clue that Luke was the one. If I found something, I would then look for more scriptures to confirm the first one. I did this on repeat for maybe three months before I had totally convinced myself that Luke was the one for me.

On New Year's eve, he called me to ask me to marry him and I could have cried with happiness. My prayers had been answered and the Christian man I knew I deserved was finally here and wanted me to be his wife.

I couldn't wait to share the news with Richard and my family. But mostly Richard. I needed to get him away from me and this seemed like the perfect way. Surely, he would have to back off now I had a 'significant other' in my life.

I don't know how Richard felt about it but he set to work trying to 'guide' me about marriage and relationships. Thankfully, I was able to reduce the amount of time we spent together because Luke was around more and more, so Richard naturally had less access to me.

Within a year, Luke and I were married and expecting our first child. We moved into our first home together, moved to a new church and gave ourselves the best chance at a fresh start with our new family.

CHAPTER 25
Soul feud

We had only been married a couple of years and Christmas was approaching. I noticed that Luke began acting very strangely and had come home from work several times, extremely drunk. So drunk he had wandered around the house naked and urinated on the floor in several places.

My husband was a Christian and I could not understand his behaviour. What made it worse was his attitude about it. He went straight to gaslighting me and made out that I was making a big deal out of nothing. He would not even apologise. I was stunned and it took all my strength and wisdom to accept that I had to forgive this offence without an apology.

I raised my concerns with our pastors who likewise did not really consider this a 'hanging' offence but equally did not offer any kind of reprimand. They gave the usual comments about marital expectations and that was that. I forgave and moved on. I thought this was an isolated incident but later realised that this behaviour was merely a symptom of something much deeper.

Little did I know that God was about to drop another bombshell!

During this same Christmas period I had spent several nights and early mornings with God. It had become a regular part of my relationship with him. It was a joy to have that uninterrupted time but the lack of sleep sometimes caught up with me.

My life was hectic. I was working full-time, studying for a degree, we had a young son, a new baby and we had only been married a couple of years. I would wake in the small hours to pray. I loved that special time with God, who would teach me, reveal things to me, ask things of me and allow me to share my deepest thoughts, worries, convictions and burdens. To this day that pattern has not changed. My night time is God's time.

Quite soon after Christmas, I was up with God and felt a particularly strong presence and a need to pray.

That night God showed me that my husband and I would be separated. This came as a bombshell. It was not just the picture he showed me but the deep emotional pain that I experienced with it.

There was nothing obvious in my marriage to suggest this would ever happen, but my soul was crushed and I cried and wept with a pain that I can hardly describe. It felt like something or someone I loved had died and the pain was almost unbearable.

I sat in my living room for many hours that night feeling a combination of shock, pain, worry and awe. This state of emotional shock lasted for around three weeks. Each night, I would silently walk downstairs to secretly cry, weep and share my deep grief.

I didn't know what to do about my marriage and decided it was best left alone. After those three weeks the memory eventually faded into the background of my mind and for a time, was forgotten.

I had always struggled with submission to my husband; Partly due to past relationships, being controlled and hurt by men, and I had a naturally dominant personality. I had prayed long and hard about this and I believe that God was helping me to change to become the wife he intended.

However, I also struggled because my husband refused to lead our family. I made most of the family decisions, planned our family time, holidays, household chores, childcare and finances. In addition, I was also our spiritual leader, initiating regular prayer, teaching our children, making sure we attended church and church activities. It was hard work and I resented having to be the driving force behind all the things I felt were important for our family.

I think my natural drive created pressure for my husband which he also resented. I expected him to be our leader, but he did not want to or was not ready to. This was a definite source of contention between us and despite my many attempts to provide support and encourage him in his role as head of our family, it was clearly futile. My husband seemed happy to follow instructions and nothing more.

Before I was married, my stepdad had been a profound spiritual influence in my life. Yet, after getting married, he was insistent about continuing in his role as my spiritual mentor.

My husband, quite rightly, objected to this and pointed out that he was my spiritual leader and not my father. (Despite his refusal to actually do it!) I was now being fought over by two men, both who wanted to control me in some way.

The situation was out of control and devolved into a face-to-face argument between my husband and my stepdad. My stepdad turned up unannounced and was on our doorstep demanding to take me from my home and spend the weekend away with him for 'spiritual guidance!'

I felt pressured to make a choice between them, not realising what a twisted situation it was. I wonder how many women are fought over like property by men?

Richard had twisted and abused Christianity to manipulate our whole family and had managed to crown himself 'king' with us as his subjects. It was easy really, as we were firm believers in the bible and we know men love to put themselves at the top of any hierarchy.

Despite the scriptures clearly saying that a man should leave his father and mother to become united with his wife. Richard was claiming that as head of his household both me and my husband should be under his authority. It was ludicrous!

It wasn't the time for a theological debate and even at the time, I remember being confused. Was this male authority meant to rule our lives?

Why would God give us conflicting instruction? Who was the boss of who? Who did I actually have to submit to? I was stressed and my stomach hurt with all the confusion over who was right and who should have control over me.

I had always believed the bible and had tried my best to submit to people in authority over me. It's what I was taught and I had no reason to question it. Yes, some people in authority abuse that authority, that was a given. However, I felt duty bound to continue to submit, even to abusive authority. This couldn't be what God wanted for me.

My choice was simple. Luke was my husband and my stepdad had no right to me, my marriage or my family, and I made sure he knew that. Even though it was stressful and I feared that at any time my husband would figure out that Richard wanted me sexually, it made me sick to my stomach.

Richard was insistent that I leave with him and both my husband and I had to threaten to remove him from our lives permanently if he would not respect our marriage. It was a gut-wrenching ordeal that I will never forget.

It wouldn't be until many years later I discovered that Richard had secretly attempted to force Luke into a subservient relationship. Trying to cast himself in the role of Luke's leader in order to continue having control and access over me.

Let me be clear. I now know that God does not call wives to submit. But he does call husbands to love and wives can choose to submit to abuse in the context of a loving relationship.

Submission is a choice born out of love. Just as Christ loves the church and does not bully, coerce or force us to obey, submit or serve. Neither should a husband. Submission absolutely should not be part of unhealthy, unbalanced or abusive relationships.

As for non-spousal relationships we are called to love one another. Not demands or expectations, or pseudo-Christian beliefs, designed to force compliance, control and abuse. This is not what the Christian faith is about and I pray that those who abuse its beliefs are one day held accountable.

I truly believed that this would mark the beginning of a fruitful change in our marriage and help my husband to become the leader I so desperately needed and wanted him to be.

CHAPTER 26
Distorted

I had finally graduated from university and the strain of study, work and family life had most certainly taken its toll. I was so happy to finally be free of the burden of my studies and glad to give time back to my family who had been neglected during my years of study.

I knew that God wanted me to change and he gave me a specific task; to take a rest with Him for forty days and gave me a list of things I needed to do.

During my forty-day rest period I was to abstain from: coffee, caffeine drinks, sugary food, snacks and drinks, stop smoking, take regular exercise, incorporate rest into my life and set aside time for prayer.

Anyone who knows me will quickly realise that the majority of this list was in complete conflict with how I lived my life. I took two weeks off work to prepare and spent them slowly cutting down on sugar, cigarettes and caffeine before I could even start my forty days of rest.

This amazing time with God taught me how to hear him clearly and built up my spiritual relationship. I took portions of my day to rest, relax, and enjoy God's presence.

During this amazing part of my journey, my husband was missing. He was there physically at home with me and the kids but his mind was elsewhere, disconnected. Despite this, my husband supported me by allowing me the space and time I needed to complete the task God gave me.

After the forty days were over, I was in a different place, mentally, spiritually and emotionally. It is like something had shifted. I don't have the exact words to describe what I felt but it was spectacular, awesome and inspiring. This is when I began to notice the change.

I began having the strangest experiences with people. Their inner person began speaking to me! At first, I did not know what was going on and thought I was losing my mind.

I would be talking with someone and be suddenly repelled by something they said. These odd conversations did not end well.

For example, I was talking with a friend and I responded to what I perceived as a very negative comment. The response from my friend was less than favourable. They became very defensive and said they had not made any such comment and why would I think that? It took me several similar conversations to realise that I seemed to be conversing with two people. Or two parts of a person at the same time.

Yes, my head was smashed and there was no one I could talk to about it. It was like I was getting two responses from people I spoke to. One from their lips and the other from their innerperson. It was extremely frightening and I started to isolate myself.

This whole thing had me completely rattled because I had no idea what was going on, or why? I began to withdraw from people, spending more time by myself to avoid this weirdness. I was scared by what I was seeing and hearing and that I might actually be crazy!

Again, this was not something that I felt I could share with my husband who had become very distant over many months. His thoughts seemed to be consumed by something that he refused to discuss. I asked him repeatedly, and prayed for openness and change but nothing seemed to make any difference. However, something happened that confirmed there was something desperately wrong.

During a marital squabble his inner person spoke to me. It spoke with venom and hate that I had never experienced from my husband before. He was a naturally placid, non-aggressive person and I saw and heard this aggressive vile thing rise out of his centre (stomach area) and begin to verbally attack and hiss at me.

I was completely stunned and frightened not knowing how to process or explain what I had experienced. I was petrified and left the family home for three days as I was too scared to stay there. I called for support from my pastors who came to talk to us. I was grateful they were there and they confirmed that what I was experiencing was a gift of spiritual discernment. This helped to dampen my fears that I was going crazy.

However, they refused to acknowledge that the marital problems were caused by anything other than a clash of our personalities. It seemed that no one else could see the things I saw. It was very isolating but I am thankful that I come from a Christian family some of whom exhibit the same or similar gifts to mine and therefore understand my predicament. We could do nothing but pray.

On my return home, things were strained but I prayerfully continued to hope that things in our marriage would change. I knew deep in my heart there was a problem and I had done everything I could to address it. But the problem remained. Without knowing what the problem actually was, I could not fix it. It was like trying to cure an unknown disease with home remedies.

Not long after this event, we made the decision that I would leave my full-time employment to become a self-employed sports instructor. I had been working towards this for many years and my employed job had become intolerable. I had a tyrant for a boss and the tension was spilling over into our home life. Change was desperately needed and we felt this was the right time to branch out.

We were both nervous about the change but we trusted that God would support and provide for us. It was a real step of faith for us financially. We had moved from a good regular income to suddenly not knowing where the work would come from or when I would get paid.

Over the next three months we became more and more in debt. My expenses soared due to extensive travel required for my new career and we tried our best to adjust to the new demands of being self-employed. My husband was completely supportive and adjusted his work hours to be at home with the children on the days when I was working early or late. For a time, it felt that our union was back on track and a new sense of partnership seemed to be growing. My fears about the problem were for a time in the background and not a major concern.

Six months later, our debts were at crisis point and we decided that we needed to overhaul our finances, change the way we lived and how we spent in order to keep our financial heads above water. This was a wonderful process that allowed me to see my husband finally take the lead on something. I stood back and allowed him to make financial decisions on behalf of our family and supported him by accepting his decisions or sharing other ideas. Although our finances were not in good shape, I felt that God was using this situation to help me practise helping my husband to become a good leader.

Unfortunately, this new found step in the right direction still seemed stilted. My husband seemed to be doing and saying all the right things but he was still as distant as ever. There was little conversation, he avoided time with me and the children, and refused to pray with me. He spent hours watching TV or was on the computer till very late at night, and we had stopped having sex. It seemed on the surface everything looked ok but underneath something was just not right.

By this time, I had run out of options, I did not know what to do, or even what the problem was. My husband refused to talk about it or even admit there was a problem, so I resolved myself to the fact that this would be my married life from now on. It's like all the life had been sucked out of my husband and despite me trying to empower him, his engine was dead.

At 8.30 a.m., my husband left for work in the morning and the family waved him off. I returned home from work after 5pm with the kids, cooked tea and waited for him to come home. At 6pm I texted him to find out when he would be back, he replied 'I have left you and I am not coming back. I hope you let me see the kids.'

CHAPTER 27
Losing at life

Shock does not even come close to the emotions I experienced that evening. At first, I was indignant and was quite proud of the fact this was the first real decision he had made in quite some time. At last, some action! This was not the action I wanted but I at least admired the fact that he was able to make a decision based on something he actually felt strongly enough about, to act upon.

This was not usual for my husband, but from the start I somehow knew that his decision was made from a position of rebellion. I don't know how I knew but I was totally convinced of this and believed God was again using my insight to show me things.

After the first week I decided it was time to tell my pastors what was going on. I had expected that they would give the usual speeches but this time it was different. We had gone through pastoral interventions so many times, and the result had been the same. Nothing changed.

My first instinct was to tell the pastors to leave my husband with his decision and allow God to do what was needed.

Unfortunately, with the usual good intentions my pastors decided that it would be better for them to make contact and help us to fix this. On an average day I would have totally agreed but this was not an ordinary day. Having asked them to intervene several times without any resulting change did not fill me with confidence.

The following weeks were filled with distressed phone calls, updates with my pastors, and explaining to every person I met where my husband was. In fact, I did not know where he was. He just disappeared and it remained that way for six weeks. It was hard enough trying to cope with this myself, let alone trying to explain to our children that daddy was not here, but I didn't exactly know where he was either.

He would not call the children despite leaving numerous messages begging him to speak to them. It was a harrowing time for our whole family. My husband's refusal to speak to me or the children to explain what was going on only made things worse.

About three weeks into his departure, I was praying, and God showed me something about mine and my husband's relationship.

Whilst I was praying God showed me and my husband walking hand-in-hand along a path. The only problem was that I was walking ahead and pulling my husband along behind me. His reluctance to walk with me acted like a brake, creating an obvious tension between us.

Realising that this was not working, I let go of his hand and started to whisper words of encouragement in his ear. After a short while he started to walk faster but soon slowed to a stumble. Then I came alongside him again and began to whisper in his ear. This repeated itself several times until I got fed-up and offered to carry him on my back.

As you can imagine, my husband is larger than me and it took a great deal of effort to hoist him onto my back and continue on our journey. I was soon exhausted and needed a rest. Once rested, I hoisted him onto my back again and continued.

This pattern continued until I was completely exhausted. I admitted defeat and told my husband I just couldn't carry him any further. With that my husband turned around, walked to a nearby tree and sat under it and I continued my journey alone.

As I mentioned before I was engrossed in my bible, prayer and various spiritual resources. I was reading 'Maximize the Moment' by T.D. Jakes (2001) and was blown away by one of the chapters titled 'When it's time to say goodbye'. Here are some excerpts by this insightful spiritual leader.

'The lack of intensity is very frustrating when a very focused, intense person is tied to someone who is less driven and more complacent. It's like trying to dance the Macarena with someone who only wants to waltz. You have one tempo for life while your partner has another. When tempos are not compatible, your energies are divided because you spend all of your much needed effort trying to motivate the partner to follow your lead and pick up the pace. You lose accomplishment eventually because you are wasting time, expecting them to be something you are not.'

'It is often a bad sign if you have to jump-start them every day. Like a car with a dry cell in its battery, if they do not hold a charge, it may be a sign of deeper trouble. You must decide if it's worth the effort to take on a life-long process of resuscitating them every week or two.'

'Without an awareness of this problem, these high-maintenance relationships can often wear you down and exhaust your strength for years. Tragically you will soon run out of your gas. In a slow downward motion, they will decelerate, because it is impossible to fuel someone else's journey from your own incentives.'

It was as if T.D. Jakes and God had been in cahoots. The words by Bishop Jakes specifically mirrored the vision God had shown me about my relationship with my husband. I knew this was how our relationship worked but I did not know why. For the first time I felt ashamed about my expectations towards my husband. What if he was never able to meet my expectations and the pressure I put on him to achieve my goals was just not possible for him?

For the first time I considered that I too had wronged him in my own way. Not through malice or hate but through the simple act of placing 'great expectations' upon a man who possibly was not able to meet them. When we feel like we have failed (and I regularly expressed to my husband that I felt he was failing me) they lose hope and motivation and begin to feel devalued as a person.

I sought forgiveness from God and sent my husband an email asking for forgiveness for any ways that I had hurt him. It was a painful but necessary healing process for me. However, it did not change the situation. But my perception of the situation changed.

When I further considered what God had shown me, it was clear that my husband had given up and despite my best efforts our future journey was not together.

My husband was already like this when we got married. However, I did not know, listen, or pay due attention to the signs. Looking back, I believe that my passion, drive and intensity for more of God, and of my marriage, placed more pressure on him than he could handle. Without knowing this (as T.D. Jakes said) there is nothing I could have done about it. And it caused further deterioration of our mis-matched relationship.

This revelation gave me a new outlook and helped me to consider that this relationship, in its current state, could not survive without Godly change. I prayed that God would do this for us and I committed to remove my expectations towards my husband and allow him to be and do whatever he needed. Despite the revelations, I still did not know why my husband left us suddenly and without explanation.

After about six weeks, my pastors had persuaded my husband to move into the church halfway house. I was unhappy about this as I felt it was further encouragement to remain away from the family home, but it was done and there was nothing I could do about it.

Early on in this episode, I felt God speak to me through the sermon about sacrifice to God. Would we be willing and what would we offer? During this sermon I felt God speak to my heart that I must sacrifice my marriage.

Sacrifice does not always mean to give up or lose something. It can also mean to submit control, let go of something and give it to another. I believed this is what God was asking me to do. To relinquish control of my marriage and this situation. Allowing him to do what was needed without fighting against him. There was an altar call at church that day and I went to be prayed for. I asked God to help me do what he had asked of me and let go.

My husband was still refusing to speak to me face to face, although there were some text messages, communication was minimal. I had also started to hear rumours from friends, church members and my pastors that my husband was accusing me of abusing him. He claimed that this had been on-going for several years and that finally he had left me because he couldn't take it anymore.

Well, imagine my surprise. I was deeply shocked and disturbed by what he said and even more disturbed by people's responses to it. It was this time that helped me see my true friends from my acquaintances.

My true friends obviously knew there was no truth to these claims but those who knew us less well, began to treat me as if I had truly wronged my husband in some way. It made me feel even more isolated, alone and unsupported than I already did. This is something church people are excellent at; judging others!

I still did not know what had caused my husband to leave, and with no communication my mind was running riot. It was not until God began to unveil the truth to me, that things finally began to start making sense.

The first of these revelations came in the middle of the night. God asked me to go and look for a necklace. A bizarre request but I have learned to do first and hold my questions when it comes to hearing from God.

I had bought my husband a gold necklace a few years before but he had only worn it for a few months before discarding it. Since then, it had lived on my bedside table for around 18 months.

After being woken by God at about 3am to search for it, I began carefully searching for it, despite it having been in plain sight previously. I searched on, under and around the bedside table, I searched all my jewellery boxes and any other places in the house it could have possibly been and did not find it.

That was the first time my mind began to contemplate what was happening. It seemed that on the day my husband left our family home he neglected to take any clothing or personal items but took a gold chain that he had not worn in over 18 months. I pondered the question and the possibilities as to 'why?'

A week later, God woke me again in the middle of the night and told me to look through my bank statements. Yes, another off the wall request. I obediently got out of bed and went downstairs to the computer to check our online bank statements.

By this time my suspicions were growing, but I had no evidence to support them. What I found shocked me to my core and sent my head spiralling. What was previously a possibility became a reality. I didn't see it straight away and was aimlessly looking through hundreds of transactions, with no idea what I was looking for. It was over an hour before I spotted the spending pattern.

I chose to search statements from the previous year but only selected four months (from twelve) at quarterly intervals. What I found sent my mind, heart and soul sinking simultaneously. Each month that I searched showed regular transactions, for small sums, in ALL the large supermarkets and chemists in the town where we lived. Every 4-6 days there were transactions at Tesco, Asda, Sainsbury's, Morrisons, Lloyds Chemist and sometimes more than one transaction per shop in the same day.

Knowing our town well, it was easy to deduce that this was an estimated ten-mile round trip to get to all those supermarkets. Another question was brewing. What was so important that he needed to visit all those shops, on the same day so regularly?

All these questions remained unanswered despite me asking and challenging my husband when I had the opportunity. He still refused to discuss anything and I was left with only my thoughts. I was starting to learn who my husband really was, and it was not nice contemplating the truth versus my past perceptions of him.

My suspicions were rooted in a life we had both left behind. We were both recovered drug addicts and had lived a crazy and destructive lifestyle, common to people like us.

I had been set free from my addiction for six years and believed that my husband was the same. However, knowing the lifestyle and mindset of an addict and the realisation that he had left with no personal belongings, but taken a valuable item that was easy to sell, left me with a sinking feeling. I later discovered he had also taken his passport, which was required at pawn shops. This was reinforced by the knowledge that weeks before, I sold an item of unwanted jewellery to get money to pay for something else.

Sometime after these initial revelations, I searched my memories to find any signs to support my suspicions. My husband had told me of his concerns about taking opiate-based painkillers for a recurring injury. I wrote down all the times I remembered and was shocked to find that God really was working with my thoughts to reveal the truth of this awful situation.

When I looked down at the list, I found that the earliest memories of my husband's disclosures were actually before we had become a couple. The disclosures covered five years! When I say disclosure, he did not outright tell me that he was addicted to opiate-based painkillers. He simply expressed a concern that he was taking them because of a fear that he may become addicted. This is the reality of being an ex-addict, we are all conscious that we can be tempted by past habits and have to maintain a life of discipline in order to reduce our exposure to dangerous elements that can trigger old behaviour.

Opium, opiates, morphine, codeine and heroin are all part of the same family of medicines and most recovered heroin addicts will not take medicines with any of these ingredients, to avoid a relapse. I had no reason to be concerned about this as my husband had recovered from his addiction for over six years (or so I thought). So whenever he brought it up, I gently reassured him that if he had pain that needed treating, he did not need to feel guilty or worried as it was for genuine medical need.

The revelations left me with little doubt that my husband had succumbed to his addiction once again. The only issue now was what would he do about it? He had already been in rehab for heroin addiction three times, so clearly there was a problem. I just could not believe how I had overlooked this for so long. I felt deceived, betrayed, foolish and alone.

The next few months were a nightmare of hearsay, lies and bad attitudes in some of the most unlikely places. I tried to seek help and advice from my pastors, friends, fellow churchgoers, my family, his family and anyone that would listen. All I succeeded in doing was alienating myself from those who did not want to believe the awful truth. Some flatly refused to believe that my loving, caring, gentle husband was even capable of this. It split my world in two. Those who believed and supported me and those who did not. My circle of friends shrank from 100% to 20%.

The impact on mine and my children's lives was devastating. We left our church because of the lack of support. We were abandoned by friends and family, and I personally felt as though I had suffered a great loss. I had already lost a husband, father and my family. Now it seemed that everything was being stripped from me. A pattern that I had seen before in my life.

It was only because I knew God had revealed the truth to me that I was able to keep going, but it was not easy.

CHAPTER 28
Finding the truth

Several months passed by and my faith that God would resolve this issue between me and my husband began to fade. I was resentful, faithless and fatalistic in my prayers. I had stopped praying for my husband to return, or that he would get swallowed into a black hole. I stopped praying that God would reveal the truth to others so I had some support. I stopped praying for a good attitude towards my husband. In fact, I struggled to pray at all and just accepted that God was going to do whatever he chose, regardless of what I prayed. I just waited in vain for him to act. I was heartbroken and spiritually destitute. I just wanted this all to end, so I could get on with my life.

It had been almost seven months without even a conversation with my husband explaining why he left. He refused to tell me the truth about his addiction (even though I already knew) and the lies he spread about me had destroyed any hope of recruiting allies to my cause.

It was during this time that God taught me about people and truth. I always knew I was different to others, even before I became a Christian. But now it seemed more than ever, that my need and desire for the truth was not the same as everyone else's.

I realised that I do not consider the truth with any emotion, whereas others do. People consider the truth as good or bad depending on their own perspective. Because of this, some people will omit the truth, bend the truth, flower the truth or avoid it, depending on how they think it will be received. I don't do that.

To me the truth is a fact that does not require any emotion. It simply is what it is. My natural tendency for blunt, frank and outspoken truth is often mistaken for rudeness, judgement or insubordination. It is none of those things to me. Truth is just a fact.

I also learned how important the truth is to me. The fact that my husband could not or would not be truthful with me, hurt so deeply and immensely that I cannot even describe it. In turn, the fact that God chose to reveal the truth to me with no clear purpose for it, left me spinning. Why tell me the truth if no one will believe it? Why torture me with the truth when I cannot use it to repair what has been damaged? Is ignorance bliss? Why did God talk to me so much, and why was he not telling anyone else what he told me?

After seven months of being absent, my husband finally contacted me to confess his addiction, express his sorrow for his actions and begin to make amends for everything that had happened. Of course, I was angry and for the first time I was able to express it. I don't want to pretend that all my time with God had somehow made me superhuman, able to forgive and forget in an instant. I am human and all the pent-up emotions that had been stuck inside for over seven months and brewing, finally had an outlet. I was honest about how I felt but hoped this would be the start of the healing process.

At first, I just listened but it was not long before I made my feelings known. Gracefully, my husband allowed me to pour out my hurt. Only when this was done, did I notice that something had changed. All this time I knew that I loved my husband. And deep down, despite everything, wanted to help him overcome whatever he was battling. However, time has taught me something. If he wanted help, he could have had it at any time!

He confessed that he had been abusing opiate-based painkillers for six years which preceded us even getting together. I was shocked and horrified to think that I had married an addict (which I always vowed I would not). Not only that, but he had lied to and deceived me into believing that he was a Godly man, who was delivered from his addictions. To find out this was not true devastated my perception of him, us, and our lives together.

He also confessed that the reason for much of the turmoil in our relationship and home was because he felt condemnation for lying and his addiction. He openly claimed he had not truly been walking with God, but that the Lord had encouraged him to contact me now. It was a lot to take in and I asked for some time to consider all the things he had told me.

This by far was the most difficult challenge I had faced. I had been on a roller coaster of a journey already and now I felt like someone had unbuckled me and I was in free-fall. There was too much going on for me to think clearly. I spent the next month having the longest, most intense and difficult conversations with my estranged husband.

None of these conversations were in-person. I did not trust myself to have a face to face conversation that would end well. We texted and emailed which gave me time to think about my responses, vent and delete where necessary and take the time to express myself in a way that was understood without being overly condemning. It was hard work and it drained me both physically and emotionally.

If there was any time for a miraculous reunion, this would have been it. But too much had happened and the hurt was too deep to be repaired overnight. I read a story in a magazine that reflected perfectly how I felt. The story went something like this.

'Truth and Lie lived and were as beings. One day Lie invited Truth for a swim in the lake. Truth accepted the invitation and they walked to the lake; undressed and got in for a swim. After a while, Lie got out without being seen and began to dress in Truth's clothing. Lie, sneaked off leaving Truth in the lake. When Truth got out of the lake and realised what had happened, he began wandering the earth searching for Lie. From that day to this, Truth wanders the earth naked, whilst Lie walks around in Truth's clothes.'

You see people find lies more palatable when they are dressed in a way that suits them. Some lies are easy to believe because they seem like the truth. But underneath they are a lie parading as the truth. When the truth is laid bare, it often offends people. No one likes nakedness; it exposes and brings shame. That is the power of the truth. However, it does not change the fact that the truth is. the truth.

This was a perfect example of the life I had been living. In my mind I had been wandering around telling the truth to anyone who would listen. Sadly, people were often offended by the harsh and ugly reality it exposed. My husband's lies were accepted, easier to believe and not challenged because those who did not value truth, found it more palatable. This is a sad truth that will never leave me. People are fickle and cannot be relied on to stand up for what is right and truthful. I will never again expect them to do so.

I had so much going through my mind that I felt I could no longer hear God clearly. I arranged to spend a week away so I could relax, refocus and get some guidance and answers from God. As usual, God did not give me the answers I wanted.

During my first few days away, I tried to relax my body and mind which was nearly impossible because of the incessant texting from my husband. I think he was aware that I was not fully committed to his return and tried everything to persuade, bully and brow beat me into taking him back. It really was not helping and I needed God to speak.

I could not trust my husband and he had done nothing to change my mistrust of him. However, the tone of the conversations became more and more pushy, condemning and downright bullying. What made it worse was he had begun preaching at me and quoting the bible to get me to take him back. It certainly felt like the pot calling the kettle black, as I was verbally abused with phrases like, backslider and white-washed Christian!

Being a Christian does not mean allowing myself to be bullied by my husband, and by day three I had had enough. I threatened that if he did not stop the constant harassment, I would cut him out of my life and there would be no reconciliation. Thankfully, he stopped and for the first time during my week away I was able to focus on God.

The same evening, I spoke to a friend who was a committed and mature Christian, to let off a bit of steam. I told her that I felt God was just not answering me and I did not know why. Her words stirred up something in me. She replied, 'If God doesn't answer my prayers, it is usually because he already gave an answer'.

The words resounded with me and I began to rack my brain trying to remember what God had told me about my marriage. I still could not remember and my friend came through again. She said, 'You told me months ago that God asked you to sacrifice your marriage'. It was like a bombshell in my soul. I had completely forgotten about that and the realisation that God still wanted me to give up my marriage, hit me like a ton of bricks. I thanked her for the conversation and put down the phone so I could continue praying.

I didn't really know what to pray for so I just prayed in tongues hoping the Holy Spirit would intercede on my behalf. After about twenty minutes, I received a very clear picture from God. I saw a length of pearl coloured ribbon, like the kind used at weddings. A large pair of silver scissors cut the ribbon into two pieces. Next I saw a beautiful and ornate bow made from the same pearl coloured ribbon. I thanked God for this picture even though I did not fully understand what it meant. I continued to pray.

The only thing I knew was that the end of the story was hope; it resonated through me as I slept peacefully for the first time that week.

The following day I felt like a weight had been lifted from me. I was happy and energetic. I used the gym facility at the hotel and spent the morning walking, praising and praying. It was the first time in months I had felt free enough to do so. I felt like the darkness had been lifted and I started feeling more like my old self.

Of course, this could have been the result of actually getting some rest and respite from living in perpetual emotional crisis. But I took it as a sign that God was doing something positive. The joy of God was rushing through me like a river and I knew that something deep within me had been renewed. I prayed for wisdom and guidance about my marriage relationship and what to do next. It was not until I was asleep that night, that God spoke to me again in a dream.

CHAPTER 29
One thing remains

I dreamed that my husband and I were in our bedroom and I was returning my wedding ring and telling him our relationship was over. He did not respond and spoke no words. I also told him that I wanted to keep my engagement ring as a keepsake to remind me of what we had; like a token of something or someone special. The engagement ring was still on my finger but when I looked down all the precious stones were missing!

My ring was a cluster of twelve diamonds with a large sapphire at its centre and sapphires set into the gold ring section, but they were all gone! It was then that I looked around the bedroom and realised that every shiny thing in the room was gone.

My son entered the room, crying, holding up a t-shirt. It was a t-shirt we had made together as part of a project. We had used sequins, diamantes and shiny objects to decorate it. All the shiny things had been stolen from his t-shirt. In fact, when I looked around the house every shiny thing had been stolen, and it was then that I saw a dark shadow rush out of the home and disappear into the night.

The dark shadow had stolen everything it thought had value. I say that because I knew it had stolen indiscriminately with no idea what had value and what was worthless. Instead, taking everything shiny, robbing our home of every precious, non-precious and beautiful thing it could find.

I then noticed that there were miniscule slivers of precious stones left in the base of my engagement ring. As I moved my hand the remaining slivers fluttered to the floor and I began frantically trying to scrape, pick and gather them up. The slivers were barely visible to the naked eye yet a desperation had come over me, as I frantically tried to save what was left of my failed marriage.

I woke up with a deeper understanding of my situation. I knew that sin had entered my home through my husband's addiction. I knew that this secret sin had silently stolen every good thing from our home and marriage. I knew that there was nothing left of our marriage to save despite my best efforts and desires. I knew that my child had also felt the devastation of this spiritual robbery. I knew that what we had was gone and there was no getting it back.

Despite the sadness, I was energised by this dream and my heart was reassured that God was showing me exactly what I needed to know so I could move forwards. I was still in the hotel. I used the internet search function on my mobile phone and began to look for scripture references to stolen jewellery, gold or treasures. I typed 'Bible – stolen jewels' and clicked on the first link at the top of the page.

What I read filled me with awe, wonder, dread and relief, all at the same time. It was a passage from Proverbs 2: 1-17. I will try and explain how I felt God speaking to me through these scriptures.

Proverbs 2: (TEV)

Verse 1 – 'My child, learn what I teach you and never forget what I tell you to do.'

This verse reminded me of the conversation I had with my friend when she reminded me of what God had told me to do earlier in the year: sacrifice my marriage.

Verse 2 and 3 – 'Listen to what is wise and try to understand it. Yes, beg for knowledge; plead for insight.'

This had been the whole point of me spending a week away. So I could seek knowledge, wisdom and insight from God to help me make the right decisions about my marriage.

Verse 4 – 'Look for it as hard as you would silver or some hidden treasure.'

This was a direct reference to my dream. I had been desperately searching and trying to retrieve what represented the tatters of my marriage. I had been seeking the wrong thing. My treasure was not in my marriage, it was in the wisdom of God.

Verse 5 to8 – If you do, you will know what it means to fear the Lord and you will succeed in learning about God. It is the Lord who gives wisdom; from him comes knowledge and understanding. He provides help and protection for those who are righteous and honest. He protects those who treat others fairly, and guards those who are devoted to him.

This is a promise fulfilled. This whole journey I had faithfully sought and devoted myself to God the best way I knew how. He filled me with his wisdom and knowledge from the start. He sent help when I needed it and he honours my honesty by using it to protect me.

Verse 9 – 'If you listen to me, you will know what is right, just and fair. You will know what you should do.'

These words weighed heavily in my heart. I was already considering what was inconceivable to my fragile human mind. Yet the decision that was forming in my heart could not be shifted.

Verses 10 and 11 – 'You will become wise, and your knowledge will give you pleasure. Your insight and understanding will protect you and prevent you from doing the wrong thing.'

This was a promise in the pipeline. Despite the tragic nature of my revelations, the proceeding decisions led to an indescribable peace. Peace in the midst of life storms and the ability to hear and follow God's direction, brought me joy that did not fit with circumstance. I should have been devastated but I was not. It made no sense and went against everything I had been taught, yet it felt good and right.

Verses 12 to15 – 'They (insight & understanding) will keep you away from people who stir up trouble by what they say, those who have abandoned a righteous life to live in the darkness of sin, those who find pleasure in doing wrong and who enjoy senseless evil and unreliable people.'

I felt like I had been hit in the head with a rock when I read these words. They were an exact description of my husband's conduct. He had stirred up trouble with his lies and deception, he abandoned us and God by running out on us all, he chose to live in his sin of addiction rather than take action to overcome it. I cannot comment on pleasure about his actions but it certainly resulted in senseless evil through the destruction of friendships, relationships and family, that need not have happened if he had only been truthful. All this results in someone who is unreliable as a spouse, father, and friend.

Verse 16 – 'You will be able to resist any immoral woman (person) who tries to seduce you with her smooth talk.'

I looked up the word immoral and found it was not solely associated with sexual misconduct.

It is also related to a person violating moral principles, lawless or who disregards rules.

I am in no doubt that the very nature of addiction and its effect on people's behaviour leads to all of the above and has certainly done so in this situation. I was devastated with the realisation of who my husband really was. The reference to smooth talk gave me shivers. I briefly touched on the point he had begun to preach at me and condemn me with scripture, for not accepting him back immediately. I was beginning to feel great pressure from him. The other thing that had plagued my thoughts was how do you know when a liar is telling the truth?

My husband had systematically lied to me and everyone we knew for over five years. He had lied to our family, friends, and pastors by portraying a devoted Christian and loving husband, which was not true. He was adept at telling people what they wanted to hear, to achieve his own ends and I had no way of telling if his words were genuine, a lie or a mixture of both. All I knew was that he wanted his old life back, and he had already shown that he would say whatever it took to get what he wanted.

He showed his true colours, by telling me that he had been diagnosed with several medical problems and was dying. He did this to pressure me into allowing him more contact with the children. This turned out to be another lie to manipulate me into doing what he wanted. God's words said I would not be seduced by such talk.

Verse 17 – 'who is faithless to her own husband (or wife) and forgets her sacred vows,'

I searched for the definition of the word faithless and found several:

- Not keeping promises, vows, or duty.

- Being untrustworthy or unreliable.

- Being without trust or belief.

- Being without religious faith.

No matter the context, all of these definitions fit. My husband had abandoned his wife, his children, his home; all financial, emotional, spiritual and practical duties towards us, and left me to pick up the pieces. My husband was faithless and did not consider his vow of marriage and commitment more than his own needs. He also abandoned God in favour of his own desires.

I cannot impress upon you how deeply this scripture penetrated my heart. It was the perfect combination of truth, revelation, understanding and wisdom. But again, it was heart wrenching, mind-blowing and unimaginable. This scripture, when considered with the dream of the stolen jewels and the vision about the cut ribbon, all came together to create a God imparted perception of my marriage situation.

The culmination of revelations over a 24-hour period, resulted in me making the biggest, and what felt like the most significant, decision of my life to date. I had a choice to make. Do I listen to what I believe God was telling me or do I rely on my own understanding?

I know all the scriptures about Godly marriage relationships but the one that stood out during this time was Mark 10:8-9 'The two shall become one flesh, so they are no longer two but one. Therefore, what God has joined together let no man separate.' My vision about the ribbon seemed a complete contradiction to this scripture and I have had this spouted at me in criticism and condemnation more than once. However, my understanding then was different.

The scripture verse speaks of man not separating a Godly union; it makes no mention of Sin causing separation or indeed of God separating. In my vision when the wedding ribbon was cut, I noticed that there was no damage to either part of the ribbon. It was not torn, ripped or burned but carefully and purposefully cut. I believe this was a representation of God separating my husband and I spiritually. The natural separation had already taken place and was caused by sin and addiction.

When people are married in the sight of God a spiritual union also takes place. In my dream I am sure that the separation of our spiritual union was God intended and purposeful. When I saw the beautiful ornate bow made from the same ribbon my heart filled with hope and joy. It was as if I knew that in order to achieve this state of beauty, the separation needed to occur.

It is like arts and crafts. You cannot make anything without cutting materials into the shapes and lengths you desire in order to create your work of art. It was like God cutting and snipping in order to create his work of art with my life. I don't know how he does it or even why. But I have faith that this separation was required in order for God to create the beauty that will shine at the end of the process.

It is this hope that outshines everything else that I have encountered. No matter the heart of my stepfather, mother, or either of my husbands. No matter the truth, lies, people's support or lack of it. I know from my very core, that this whole process brings with it the hope of beauty.

I cannot shake it off and I have no intention of being sad or downhearted because of my loss. God has given me hope in the midst of my life storm. He has revealed his heart and his truth. He has protected me, shared his wisdom and given me guidance and counsel. He is my very best friend and nothing can separate me from him, nor him from me.

I am in the midst of my greatest test of faith. Do I act on what I believe God has revealed to me? The answer is a resounding yes. Am I worried that I could be wrong? No, I am not worried about being wrong. I know that for every failure God is more than able to do good work through it. I know that every decision is temporary and has the ability to change at a moment's notice.

Many years ago, God showed me a picture to help me understand the difference between human thinking and the way God thinks.

Human thinking is like light through a pane of glass – it only has the ability to go in and out one way.

God's thinking is like light being shone through a multi-faceted diamond that has an infinite number of surfaces for the light to reflect off.

God is able to see how the light reflects through all and each refraction of the diamond. Following the trail of light through multiple paths and destinations, all at once. His thinking is higher, greater and deeper than we can even imagine. Therefore, how can we claim to know what God thinks, unless he reveals it to us?

There is no question...my trust is in God, and God alone.

Jeremiah 29:11

"For I know the plans I have for you," declares the LORD, "plans to prosper you and not to harm you, plans to give you hope and a future."

Amen

www.marciampublishinghouse.com